Lock Down Publications and Ca$h
Presents

HUNGRY FOR MONEY

24 Seconds

By

SLIMBOS

First Edition 2024

Printed in the United States of America

Lock Down Publications
P.O. Box 944
Stockbridge, GA 30281
www.lockdownpublications.com

Like our page on Facebook: Lock Down Publications
www.facebook.com/lockdownpublications.ldp

Stay Connected with Us!

Text **LOCKDOWN** to 22828 to stay up-to-date with new releases, sneak peaks, contests and more…

Like our page on Facebook:
Lock Down Publications

Join Lock Down Publications/The New Era Reading Group

Visit our website:
www.lockdownpublications.com

Follow us on Instagram:
Lock Down Publications

Email Us: We want to hear from you!

Table of Content

Chapter 1

Cee Money was only twenty-two years old, but she ran circles around those sucka duck ass niggas like a game of Duck Duck Goose. She had her own spot in Phenix City, Alabama, so she was able to keep taps on all the hood gossip in Columbus since she was only seconds away. The Chattahoochee River was the only thing separating the two states. Furthermore, those clowns put all their business on social media. They were so thirsty to impress a bad bitch, so all she had to do was make herself available. She wasn't even from Columbus or Alabama, yet she knew everything that was going on because she was born money hungry.

A hard life in Albany, Georgia caused her to develop a black heart at the earliest age. She never had time to be a normal, Black, little girl. Her upbringing was cruel and unusual. Her daddy was a functional junkie, and her mother was a seasoned whore. She had an older brother and a few sisters, but she was the demon of the bunch. Nobody was there when that thirty-four-year-old, R. Kelly ass nigga took advantage of her, but everyone always called her for help. She hated herself for being so naïve, but she had to be the superhero for her family's sake.

"Cee Money, do you hear me? I said did I leave my keys in the kitchen?" asked her mother, Trina, bringing her back to reality. She was thinking about how she was going to pick up her man from Smith State Prison tomorrow morning and could not stop smiling until she heard her mother yelling at the top of her lungs.

"I don't fuckin know. Damn. Leave me the fuck alone!" Cee Money responded with an attitude.

Before her mother could steal her attention again, her iPhone started ringing, and Rednose appeared on the screen.

"Hey, baby, why the fuck you ain't answering your phone? Nigga, you must be on the phone with your other hoes?" She was so damn toxic.

Smith State Prison was the worst prison in Georgia. No, the worst in the United States. Hell, probably the worst in the world. So, Rednose was very excited to finally be getting released tomorrow morning. He was so anxious that he could not even sleep. All of his long list of things he had planned, he could now finally put it together. Most were good, but a lot were evil. Because Rednose often had battles within himself, his anxiety caused him to develop a mental illness called explosive disorder. He would randomly explode out of nowhere from time to time. Then, he would go right back to talking righteous and positive as if nothing had happened. Yeah, he was a whole nutcase. However, the things he had been through in life caused this. Some would say he was bipolar, but he denied all of those allegations. He would say, "I'm not crazy. Y'all motherfuckers are crazy!"

He had been lied to, robbed, stolen from, crossed out, stepped on, ran over, and deceived so much in his thirty-two years on Earth. If a person was a good person, he normally would run them off with his anger issues. He didn't trust anybody. "Absolutely not," was how he responded when the voice in his head would say, "Give them a chance. They might be okay."

His mother and sister had both stolen money from him since he'd been in prison. Every female he trusted would run off with his money that he'd run up hustling when he was on compound at Smith State Prison. In 2020, he ran up a couple grand and didn't know how to act. He was giving money out so freely that he didn't have time to put anything up for himself.

"That Cash App got closed."

"My screen cracked. I can't press send," or, "My dog ate my homework." You name it, he heard it all, every excuse in the book. So, it was clear in his mind that you couldn't trust anyone as far as you could throw them. When he lost trial and was found guilty, everybody — and I mean everybody — left him for dead!

So, his heart was just as cold as theirs. Even in prison, his own gang threw him under the bus out of jealousy and envy. They put out a bunch of false allegations and spread rumors with ill intent to destroy his image and reputation. They'd cancelled him off of compound four years ago, so he had been on compound restriction since then. They did this to leave him for dead to rot. He had been living in the box in bondage for almost half a decade, knowing that on twenty-four seven lockdown that he couldn't get any motion going on to attempt to fight his case or make any money to buy a lawyer to help him on appeal. Yeah, people were evil and ruthless as fuck, but somehow, he still prevailed against all odds.

Rednose wasn't getting out of prison broke. Not only did he beat the odds, but he also ran up $25,000 that he had stashed in his Underdog Fantasy account.

This was a brilliant move by him. For one, nobody could touch his money but him. Nobody knew his Gmail information or password to his account. Past experience had sharpened his mind when it came to financial management. He wasn't the type of inmate to sit on his cell phone all day on social media. Nawl, he was on the hunt. He was definitely on a serious paper trail. God blessed him with a natural gift of gab that he used to better his situation every chance he got.

The only time he would get on social media would be to post his daily stories on Facebook, which only lasted twenty-four hours. That was how he would shoot his shot. He came up with a clever way to determine whether he was wasting his time. For example, whoever viewed his story, he would inbox. If that person left him on read, he would immediately block them.

"How they got time to read my message but not respond? But they watch all my stories? Something ain't right, G! Either they are the police, a catfish, or a person trying to set me up!" He would yell out loud to no one in particular as he blocked them.

On the positive side however, the ones who responded, he would simply say small, nice things and keep it going. They had no idea he was acting as an agent. He was like Rich Paul, looking to sign the best person in the draft pool to help rebuild his franchise. He only needed one point guard, one female who was young, with no kids, and right in the middle of the culture. It wasn't easy, and she was definitely not going for any regulation, chain gang, fast talking. But one day, he found her, and their chemistry had been damn near perfect since the first conversation. She could see through all the bullshit, and she was dead serious about money. So, he gave her the nickname Cee Money.

"You think I got time to entertain a bum right now? I'm getting this business license and shit together."

"Baby, you tripping. Fuck all them hoes! Can't nobody take your spot. Where them hoes was at when I was broke?" Rednose snapped back at Cee Money as he paced back-and-forth inside his small cell.

He wasn't lying to her, but he wasn't telling her everything either. Together over the last seven months, the two of them had been in sync. They gave "money hungry" a new meaning. They had two cars that were paid off sitting in her driveway. He had his own place, and she had her own spot. They both agreed it was best not to move in together as soon as he came home from a ten-year prison bid. She kept all the money they had made together in different accounts.

They never put all their eggs in one basket. Rednose never put all his trust in one person. She wasn't aware of the twenty-five grand he had ducked off in his Underdog Fantasy account, and he had suspicions but didn't put too much thought in it about money she had that she didn't say anything about.

They both had individual plans they kept to themselves and also plans they made together. Cee Money wanted to be rich. Rednose wanted to be wealthy. He felt like prison had robbed him out of a billion-dollar career. So, he was entering the game down 28-3 at halftime. So, he was always in "Tom Brady Mode."

Cee Money saw her parents and siblings barely making it and always begging for her help, so she told herself she would never go broke again. When she was broke before, nobody helped her, but those same people were always giving victim type testimonies when they needed something. She refused to turn her back on her family, so she played the superhero role even when she wasn't feeling the situation.

The two of them wanted to move to the west coast, so Rednose could pursue his career. Meanwhile, Cee Money wanted to join the military and pursue her career.

The plan sounded good, but there was so much that had to be done before they could make it out of the death trap called "The New Columbus, GA."

Rednose had seen a lot of guys around his age get out of prison and either get locked up or murdered in sixty days. It happened so much that it was expected by now. Older guys came home with that prison mentality. Younger guys in the city were not going for that bullshit. Period.

Rednose had been at Smith State Prison for so long that he was very familiar with the staff. He knew every count of every dorm and every count of every officer on every shift. The prison was so understaffed that it was a shame. Maybe that was why so many inmates got killed. It seemed like someone was getting stabbed every day, and out of ten stabbings, someone would bleed to death due to inadequate medical treatment.

Rednose recalled one time when two roommates had a knife fight inside their cell. No officer was inside the building or inside the control room. Imagine fighting for your life, knowing that if you didn't kill the person, you would more than likely bleed to death waiting seven to thirteen hours before an officer would come around to check on you. Most of the officers didn't even care or take it seriously. During this particular incident, the inmate that died was stabbed over fifteen times and bled out for over four hours before help finally arrived. So, was he murdered by his roommate? Or did he die because of the breach of security and deliberate indifference the staff displayed under clearly established law? The failure to protect combined with the inadequate medical treatment was indeed the true killer. That was why Rednose went to sleep with his weapon and never let it get out of his reach. He didn't trust any of his roommates because they were all convicts with ulterior motives.

So, on the morning he was released from prison, all the fake kicking it began. Certain inmates who'd never liked him came to his dorm and ran up to his door with fake congratulations speeches.

"You gave back a life sentence, brah! You the goat!" Blah, blah, blah.

These same inmates had been oppressing him since he was put on compound restriction. When he was on compound, niggas were scared to play with him, but when he was behind the door, niggas tried all types of shit. Being the person he was and a Scorpio, he promised to get revenge by putting that cheese on those niggas' heads like a Green Bay Packers fan.

"All them fuck niggas gonna die!" he reminded himself daily.

He did something unusual the morning he was released.

"Officer, I'm not coming out my cell until y'all lock all the orderlies down. I fear for my life. They trying to kill me before I make it out the gate. It's a hit on me!"

Puzzled but seeing the look on his face, the officer called his O.I.C., and almost two hours later, Rednose was escorted to the front gate by six members of the task squad, and the south side of Smith was placed on emergency lockdown. All the inmates with details were sent back to their dorms.

"Nigga, what the fuck took you so damn long?" Cee Money was both nervous and excited when Rednose finally walked with confidence toward her Hellcat.

After he explained what he did and why, she couldn't help but laugh but understood the wisdom behind it.

"Man, you do the most, brah."

The two were caught up, staring each other down for a moment.

Cee Money was a natural beauty with a hardcore edge to her. You could tell she didn't wear dresses and shit like that, but she was fine as fuck — brown skin and thick with some small breasts. Her hair was on fleet, and her shoe game was lit. She had a few tattoos that enhanced her beauty. Her face was pretty. She had some dark brown eyes and cute dimples. He couldn't believe she didn't have any kids. He knew he was about to go clap that lil shit up for a few hours as soon as they got to her spot.

Meanwhile, she was also checking out her man that she helped break out the system. Rednose was tall and had a slim but toned body. He was light skinned with light brown eyes. He had tattoos everywhere and wore his hair in a high temp fade. He always looked mean, but when he saw her, he displayed his smile and undercover positive side. She knew he was just a jellybean — hard on the outside and soft on the inside. She knew he deserved this new chance at life and was happy to share it with him, but she would shoot him with no hesitation if he played with her feelings because she'd shot a nigga before and would do it again. But as long as they were getting money, everything was going to be okay. Well, that was what the plan was. In life, we all knew plans never went through without any type of turbulence. When you were getting money, you were also getting a lot of problems.

But those problems were different. Rednose was on a revenge tour, and he thought he was going to get out and just take over, but Cee Money knew she had to prepare him for a different outcome. That was the conflict she was already expecting, but she did not expect it to happen as soon as it did.

"Twirl on dat dick. Hell yeah, bounce on it real slow, just like dat. Keep dat back straight. Keep dem legs open. Shit, girl, I'ma fuck around and cum all in this good pussy. I didn't know you was flexible like this." Rednose was popping his shit as Cee Money showed him how her pussy worked.

They had been at it for some days now. She would wake him up with that bomb ass head game. She could switch it up nice and slow or nasty and fast. She let him clap dat phat thing from the back and wrapped her legs around him when he turned her ass to pound town from the buck position.

Rednose was mostly in love with the way she rode his dick like a freak. This girl was flexible like a young Ciara but freaky like a porn star on some Perocets.

Her pussy juice made his thrust sound off with each stroke. She wasn't really a moaner, but he could tell she enjoyed the way he worked his hips and kept up with her young, hot ass. Rednose was ten years older than her, but they were very compatible.

"Ohh weee. Baby, I'm cummin again. Damn, dat dick feel so good to me!" she whispered while creaming all over his tip.

While she rocked her hips and bounced up and down on his dick, he rubbed her clitoris with his thumb and index finger, causing her to go crazy.

After she came, he immediately used his strong arms to pick her up and sit her on his face. He had to taste that creamy, juicy pussy just to make sure he wasn't dreaming. The way this young girl had him feeling was so surreal and amazing. He couldn't believe he'd actually done ten years with no pussy. At that moment, he knew he would die before he went back to prison. Those days were over and done with.

"Damn, bae, you just going to stick your whole tongue in my bootyhole like dat?" she asked in a low, seductive voice. She even looked back at him with a naughty grin on her cute face.

Her back was shining from her sweet body sweat.

Rednose was a freak. He licked her butthole and fingered her pussy. Then, he would eat her pussy out and stick a finger inside her booty. She never had anyone do her this good, but she wasn't about to gas this nigga up by telling him this. Rednose knew she was shaking because he was tapping that G-spot. She had to put her hands on the wall behind the headboard to keep her balanced. That boy knew how to suck on dat cat.

When he tasted her cum, he finally let her back down and sat up, smiling like he just hit the jackpot.

"What you smiling about, nigga? You ain't did nothing!" Cee Money laughed before she jumped up and strutted toward the shower. Her nice, phat ass cheeks jiggled with each step.

"Got damn, that lil ass phat!" Rednose yelled out with excitement.

"Boy, stop staring at my booty and you a freak. You been fucking me all weekend, man. You be cumming so hard... Shit!" Cee Money exclaimed as she turned on the shower water.

"Well, baby, I got some big ass nuts for one, and I'm backed up like hell, so I'ma be beating that pussy up every day for the next few months," Rednose announced with confidence as he scrolled through his Android.

"No the fuck you are not, sir. We got to get to the money, and I'm not ready to get pregnant, so you need to stop cumming inside me, nigga. I told you not to do it, but you still keep trying me!" Cee Money cried from the shower. She loved him with all of her heart, but she wasn't ready to fully commit, not just yet. Plus, they had a whole plan that didn't warrant a baby being involved.

Her thoughts were interrupted when he snatched the shower curtain back and stood tall and naked, looking her in her eyes. "Who the hell you yelling at? I'm not in prison no more, girl. I'll choke your ass out!"

Rednose pushed her against the shower wall, put light pressure on her neck, and stuck his tongue in her mouth before she could protest. Cee Money tried to put up a fight, but her body was weak for him already.

They made love again inside the shower before they got clean and finished up. Next, they sat at the roundtable to discuss business plans. The city of Columbus, Georgia was about to be hit by a massive storm, a massive tornado, that was going to spin throughout the entire city.

Before Rednose went to prison, he was basically the young OG around town. At twenty-two years old, he had put over thousands of people under his training and plugged them. He was even on their asses about going to school and smoking. He would constantly encourage them to play sports or hop in the studio and make music. Being ninety miles south of Atlanta, Columbus was like a smaller version of ATL. But Columbus had its own style. They even had a dance that went viral in 2015 called *Hit Dem Folks Up*.

Rednose was locked up when it went viral, but he knew it was worldwide when he saw Odell Beckham, Jr. and Cam Newton doing it. He was salty at first because people from ATL were taking credit for it and trying to switch it up and make it look weird and not original.

Rednose was the first rapper from Columbus to start a three letter gang as a local rap group and street team to promote his music. He had members from all over town and even across the bridge in Phenix City that were all repping the same brand. He was also the first one to do that as well. So, when he went to prison and finally got a cell phone, he was able to see the lack of respect and appreciation from some of the younger guys who used to follow him around like little puppies. They had basically stolen his whole image and ideas and recreated it to fit the new generation.

"These fuck niggas ain't sent me a dime or shout a nigga out or nothing! And all of them have flipped and switched to a different gang! Where the fuck they do that at? Disloyalty!" he would say during the time he got caught venting or sounding like he was hating.

Notwithstanding, they also had some weird stuff going on. For example, the most popular group of guys that he used to be around the most were all beefing with each other and on two different sides of town now. However, you had people playing both sides and setting each other up. You had two oppositions teaming up on a common enemy. So, when he would reach out to one side, the other side felt like he was playing both sides of the war.

"Nigga, I don't pick sides. I'ma real gangsta. Y'all niggas on some hoe shit out here! All y'all used to be in the same gang; now y'all got y'all own gang, and y'all beefing with each other! That shit weird and confusing. So, fuck all y'all pussy niggas! Y'all ain't sent me nothing my whole bid! None of y'all fuck niggas! I was just reaching out like a concerned older brother, fuck nigga! I got my own money, pussy! I'll be home soon, and when I do, I'ma knock all y'all fuck niggas off!"

That was how Rednose talked to himself when he would be doing push-ups or squats in his cell. He was mentally ill like that. Explosive disorder.

So, if you hadn't figured it out by now, Rednose was going to reclaim his spot as the top dawg in the city by simply eliminating all these new gangs of street punks. They were so sweet. All they did was post all their money on social media like a real monster wasn't in the cut, ready to pop out and kidnap the prey and hold him hostage, tied up, and put him in the back of his own truck for a few days. They didn't see or know he was coming. A force that could not be seen could not be stopped.

The most popular group was signed to a millionaire up in Atlanta. He would get them last because he needed more information and the perfect timing.

Nobody knew he was out of prison because he didn't post anything on social media, and Cee Money was the only person that knew he was home. He planned to surprise his mother and baby sister in a few days, but he had to go put some shots up at the shooting range and get the rust off first thing in the morning. Also, he had to go and try out some new weapons that were popular these days. Nobody used those weapons from ten years ago anymore. The good thing about Rednose having a cell phone on lockdown the last few years of his bid was that he was able to learn and observe a lot of information that would be very important.

"So, what we doing tomorrow, baby?" Cee Money asked Rednose as they ate hot food off of plates with silverware, something he cherished now.

"After we go get my driver's license renewed, take me to that gun range you and your sister be going to. I'm kinda rusty. Then, we going to deal with Carlos." He said it so casually, like they were going shopping or something.

"What the fuck, man? You crazy. You only been out a few weeks, and you talking about going on a drill already!" yelled Cee Money. "Can we at least go shopping or stay put up a few more weeks before we pop out on that hitman bodyguard ass shit?" She continued to protest.

"Okay, okay, baby. Damn, stop crying! Carlos made it personal, so that fuck nigga gonna die slow." Rednose smiled, but it was a cold one.

Carlos had recently robbed Cee Money while she was serving him, which caused her to stop trapping all together. When Carlos took her gun out of her purse, she knew it was over with, so she looked at her iPhone and yelled, "Rednose, I'm getting robbed! Call my sister!"

All Rednose remembered was Carlos saying, "What his pussy ass going to do? Nothing! He stuck in prison for life! I should fuck the shit out you and send him the video, bitch!" Then, the call disconnected. Yeah, it was personal.

"Okay, baby. Let's stay put up for a few more weeks, but it's business after that! Once we start, ain't no slowing down. I'ma knock these lil fuck niggas off so fast; then, we up out this small ass city. All these niggas having all this motion don't even know they about to get knocked off they lil high horse."

Chapter 2

So, when you came home from prison, you were supposed to be rewarded? You thought the city you did so much for would be happy that you were back? No, it didn't work like that! Never had. Those first few weeks was just a bunch of fake love and guilt tripping. That was why Rednose decided not to tell a soul he was back home.

He had been moving very discreetly and mysteriously. The only time he left Cee Money's spot was to handle business and get things done. He even pushed back the assassin on Carlos a few months. He also decided that his mother and sister could wait a few months before they knew he was home as well. It was not like they were going to call the prison to check on him anyway.

Rednose may have been the only inmate to sneak a cell phone out of prison. Yeah, he kept his phone for two reasons. One, so if anybody called, he could play the role like he was still in the box on compound restriction. And reason two was because he didn't want to leave anything to any of those ungrateful ass fuck niggas. He was still traumatized and couldn't wait to inflict gruesome pain on his opponents. And that was about to begin. His personal welcome home party.

Two people had to die first that did not even involve the original plan. Carlos and Mook. As you knew, Carlos had robbed and put his hands all over Rednose's queen, and he added insult to injury by boasting with foolish arrogance, thinking Rednose was stuck for life in bondage. For that, he would die a slow and brutal death. He committed a double violation in one.

Now, Mook was another personal matter. Rednose and Mook had been cool since they were around twelve or thirteen. Mook used to be a dirty, broke, fat boy running behind the popular people in the hood on the south side. Rednose used to rotate from the east side of town and the south. Ironically, he was popular on both sides, so he naturally made haters and enemies. The difference between haters and enemies was simple. Enemies just flat out let it be known that they didn't like you and hated with no regard. Haters played cool with you for a certain amount of time just to copy you and collect information on you to go gossip about it and use it against you in the future. They even followed you on social media but didn't like anything but watched everything, too jealous to show love and too nosy to unfollow. Mook was a hater since day one that became an enemy and a snake. Now, if you didn't know what a snake was, you deserved to get bitten.

Mook used to say things like, "Oh, hell nawl. You just gave that nigga some pussy, and he not even from the hood!" when Rednose used to come on the south side and fuck all the hood rats that Mook had been trying get at. Then, when they got older, Mook ended up in the same gang as Rednose but didn't have as much of an impact with recruiting as Rednose. Mook was a major factor and had plenty of people fooled like he was a real one. But he grew greedy for domination, and respect brought out the snake in him.

Rednose and Mook ended up at the same prison, inside the same dorm. They bumped heads in every way. From the outside looking in, you would think it was just some homeboy love type shit going on, but one man was just simply jealous of the other. What one man wanted, the other had without even trying.

This outraged Mook to the point that he used his power in the gang to put false rumors and charges against Rednose, which led to Rednose getting blackballed by his own gang. Mook was selling some of the same drugs Rednose was but didn't tell that part. He just ratted Rednose's dirt and flaws out to hide his own flaws and jealousy. Not only that, but Mook knew Rednose was fighting a life sentence and couldn't get any access to law materials while being placed on compound restriction. He knew what the charges and allegations would do to Rednose — hinder him and sabotage his reputation. So, of course, he took credit for it every chance he got.

"I'm the one put that nigga off compound. Fuck Rednose. That nigga stuck on compound restriction forever!" He would often boast when he got the chance.

Mook destroyed Rednose's street credibility, financial opportunities, and subjected him to cruelty and harsh living conditions. For that, he would pay with his life. Rednose was so serious about this premeditated murder. He even blocked Mook and everyone connected to him on all social media sites, so nobody could stalk or have any clue about Rednose's movement. They didn't know if Rednose was broke, had a cell phone, on drugs, depressed, still fighting a life sentence, or in a vehicle trailing right behind Mook. A force that could not be seen could not be stopped.

"Him and this nigga got hit up the same night, but I caught 'em separate." Rednose quoted lyrics from a young rapper from Memphis but substituted *we* for *l* as he drove in an unmarked vehicle. He was dressed in all-black with a hoodie and a black COVID mask covering most of his face.

Currently, he was trying to catch Mook at a red light or stop sign or something, but this nigga ran all traffic lights. It was hard as fuck to keep a trail on him, especially with the rain pouring down on a Friday evening. But Rednose managed to stay close enough not to lose sight of the prey. He was in pure hunter mode. Yeah, he was a monster on the hunt for not one but two separate kills in one drill.

He knew upon research and study that Carlos was at a low-key bowling alley on a date with his girl and their daughter on the north side.

Rednose originally planned to get at Carlos first, but Mook suddenly fell in his lap, and it went a little something like this.

While waiting on Carlos to come out the front entrance, he logged in his catfish account on social media, making sure to keep his location off. He noticed a notification announcing that Mook was going live. So, he immediately viewed the live stream.

It was, in fact, Mook in the car with two females, taking shots and grinning like a virgin finally about to get some pussy. The fact that Mook was going live didn't surprise him. He had been going live every day like a motherfucker was not planning his death date out. The thing that surprised Rednose was that Mook was only a few exits away. The sudden urge to blitz the traffic jam he was stuck in, taking shots, was too much of an adrenaline rush to resist.

Now Rednose had to hurry. If he wanted to catch Carlos, he needed to hope Mook stopped at one of these stop signs or red lights. It took him about seven minutes to reach the location Mook was at and another five minutes for the car Mook was in to bypass him, so he could follow it, and he had now been in pursuit for a couple minutes. With his left hand on the wheel and right hand gripping his Glock with the switch, Rednose began to panic. His anxiety had him anxious and thinking he would miss Carlos because of chasing Mook as the car led him farther and farther away from the direction Carlos was in.

"This nigga don't stop at red lights at all, brah. WTF wrong with this nigga?!" Rednose was getting frustrated and began talking to himself. After another five minutes, he was about to say fuck it until Mook did something unusual. He stopped at a traffic light for a brief moment, but as soon as Rednose put his car in park and was about to hop out and flip the switch, the nigga hit the gas again, running yet another red light.

"Damn, I almost had that fuck nigga!" Rednose yelled out to himself. He was about to end the pursuit and race back to the location Carlos was in until Mook turned into a local gas station.

"Ohh, shit, this nigga sweet!" Rednose sped up and immediately parked in the lot right across from the gas station.

He hopped out and kept his head low as he proceeded to walk down on that boy.

Mook had hopped out and walked in the convenience store to buy whatever the fuck it was that he wanted as the two ladies stayed inside the vehicle. Rednose was on the side of the store and knew he had an easy kill. At least he thought so. So, as Mook stepped outside, he lifted his Glock and let it rip.

Blah! Blah! Blah! Blah! Blah! Blah!

Mook dropped like a sack of potatoes. "Yeah, fuck nigga, SW can't save yo bitch ass now!" Rednose yelled out and was about to finish the nigga off when, suddenly, the doors of the car Mook was driving swung open.

Both females had assault rifles and were aiming at Rednose.

"Drop yo gun, pussy!" one of them yelled. Rednose knew he had slipped and rushed into some crash dummy shit because he reacted out of emotion instead of logical thinking. All he had to do was be patient and catch Mook another day, but his anger caused him to make a poor decision. He thought he saw everything in the car from the live video but didn't see these two Dracos or expect those lil slut looking hoes to be some shooters!

Rednose quickly glanced at Mook and saw he was bleeding badly from his neck area. He thought about aiming at the female who was talking, but the one who wasn't talking was staring directly at him with death in her eyes, and her silence was scary. Then, something strange happened. Another group of females drove by the car the females had been in and rolled down the window.

"There go them hoes who set up my brother right there!" was all Rednose heard before Christmas shots were fired from the vehicle, instantly dropping the female who'd told Rednose to drop his gun. But the other female was backpedalling and returning fire like she was on *Call of Duty* or something. Rednose was definitely impressed but took that chance to get the fuck out of there, leaving Mook to continue to bleed out. He could hear the female shootout as he raced to his car and drove away. He was nervous, angry, and excited all at the same time. He had never experienced something so intense that had the power shift three different ways in what seemed like only a moment.

"Boy, I almost got my shit pushed back!" Rednose yelled as he sped through traffic en route back to Carlos' location.

The fact that he'd just shot Mook and was nearly shot only made him more desperate for a kill. He didn't know if Mook would make it or not, but from all the blood, he would probably die right there on the pavement.

"I wonder why them hoes ain't pop my top though?" Rednose was puzzled at the fact that the bitch told him to drop his gun instead of getting revenge for him walking down on Mook. He figured after some thought that the one who was talking wasn't a killer for real, but the other one looked like she was dangerous and even knew how to work that Draco and dodge fire. *She must been a military hoe or something,* he thought.

All those thoughts left his mind when he arrived back at the bowling alley and noticed Carlos putting his daughter in the backseat as his baby mama got inside the passenger seat.

"Oh, fuck no. Not again!" he expressed as he drove directly behind their car and smashed the brakes like a crazy man.

Carlos was blinded by the headlights but instantly reached for his hip, but he was not fast enough.

"Hands up, fuck boy! The fuck you reaching for, buddy?" Rednose disarmed Carlos and aggressively forced his face to the ground.

"Help! Stop! Please! What are you doing? You crazy!" was all the baby mama could yell out of pure fear and shock as she watched helplessly. Rednose duct taped and tied up her baby daddy so fast and viciously that she knew this wasn't his first time doing this. If she was smart, she would have called the cops or ran and got some help. What made it worse was that the child was in the backseat crying for her daddy.

Chapter 3

A few weeks later, Rednose was in the gym, putting in work. He usually got it in four days out of seven. On the weekends, he went to the basketball gym and put up shots. He would put up about five hundred shots between Friday and Saturday. Today, he wasn't going to the basketball gym once he finished banging in the weight room. He was going to surprise his queen, Cee Money. He had not seen her in weeks. They hadn't talked on the phone in days, and she had not texted him since the day before yesterday.

"Think I'm going to surprise my baby today. I miss her toxic ass," Rednose said as he jumped in his car and sped off blasting Future.

He took a hot shower and shaved up good. When he was finished, he put on his favorite cologne and got fresh in a new fit before he jumped back in his whip and hit traffic.

He started to text her and let her know he was on his way, but something nice came to him. He changed directions and went to the nearest place to buy some flowers, cards, and candy to impress his queen. She probably thought he had been out with other freaks, but that was not the case at all.

Actually, he had been trying to get his mind right after how things went back when he decided to spin on Mook and Carlos. So, he had been at his spot, fasting and in deep meditation. He had been talking to his ancestors and making offerings for forgiveness.

"I'ma make my good outweigh my bad, but it's a lot of niggas going to die before I do more good," he admitted to himself frequently.

According to the news outlets and social media platforms, Mook had survived and was hospitalized. However, he was later arrested for violating his probation after being questioned about the double homicide that took place at the gas station involving the female shootout.

There were a lot of different stories going around. Rednose had to go into private investigator mode to separate the real scoop from the fake tea being spilled. This generation was full of snitching, whether on purpose or accidentally. All you had to do was stay in the loop by keeping your ears and mouth open. So, once Rednose concluded his findings, he drew out this assessment.

The female who'd told him to drop his gun was shot dead on the scene, while the other female was on the run currently. The reason she was on the run was because another female, that was in the other car that had pulled up shooting, was killed as well. A few more were injured, but the rest of the details were still fuzzy. Rednose knew that lil bitch was a real shooter just by the way she wasn't talking when the other one was yelling at him and from how she returned fire at the vehicle that shot at them. Mook's pussy ass was just lucky, but Rednose would wait for another chance to get him. This time, he would move smart, not driven by anger.

In other news, Carlos was still missing, according to Rednose's private investigating. The baby mama's description of how he was kidnapped by a man with all-black, who wore a mask to conceal his face, sounded like something out of a movie. It was scary how she told the story. It was like a new serial killer was on the loose or something. People all over social media were posting the hashtag #WhereIsCarlos. Unfortunately, no one knew besides the monster, Rednose.

So, he had to lower his vibration and chi before he could go back around Cee Money. Trying to explain this to her was not possible, so he was just going to pop up and attempt to charm her and hand out gifts. He knew she would have an attitude but would not deny him.

When he pulled up, he noticed a red SRT backing out of her driveway. When the car passed him, the clown ass nigga driving had the nerve to stare him down like Rednose was too small or something. This instantly made Rednose angry and very suspicious.

"The fuck you looking at, pussy?!" Rednose yelled out the window with malice.

However, the guy just had a cheesy grin plastered on his black ass face before he sped off.

Rednose pulled in the driveway behind Cee Money's green Hellcat with the tinted windows. It wasn't until he was knocking on her door that he realized he did not have a key to her spot. Then, he began to think of all kinds of other things he didn't know about Cee Money. The longer she took to open the door, the madder he got.

"Hey, baby," was all she said. Then, she walked inside the living room, leaving the door open. Rednose placed the flowers and gifts on the kitchen table before he followed her inside the living room.

"Nigga, you think you can just disappear for damn near a month then pop up with some flowers and shit! What the fuck do you take me for?" Cee Money snapped with a loud attitude, jumping all in his face.

Rednose just looked at her. *This bitch funny*, he thought. He could tell she was used to running over niggas, and she thought she was smarter than him, and it was actually funny to Rednose. He decided to let her get it off her chest.

"You haven't called or texted me back. I been blowing you up, and I know you been fucking a bitch. You think this shit funny, but I'll do something to you for real, boy. I'm the one that rode with your ass while you was stuck in a cell all day, and I helped you get that lawyer money up, so how dare you disrespect me like this?" Cee Money rolled her eyes and started crying.

Either she was the greatest snake ever or she was genuinely upset. Rednose was so confused that he almost forgot about the guy that had just left her house before he came, but he decided to play it cool for the moment.

"And I seen you being all rude to my friend who just left from over here. Don't do it again because we do business together, so if you not trying to slow up my money, please respect my company and clients. You can't just pop up and get aggressive with a person you don't even know!" Cee Money exclaimed then went into the kitchen to examine and touch her flowers and gifts. She tried to hide her smile before she walked in her bedroom.

Rednose knew she was going to be acting funny, so he had to spice things up a little bit more. He heard her turn on the shower and turn on her music. She loved Sza. As Cee Money took off her clothes and stepped into the shower, she could hear things moving around her kitchen. She shaved her legs and stomach hair because she knew what time it was with Rednose back. She had no need to shave her coochie hair because she kept it waxed.

When Cee Money got out of the shower and was dressed, she walked in the kitchen and was surprised to see Rednose cooking a whole meal and had it smelling good as fuck to her delight. She came up to him and wrapped her arms around his waist. She let her head rest on the back of his neck. She couldn't help it. She was so in love with this man.

"So, I'm your little bitch now? Got me cooking for you while you come get behind me and shit?" Rednose joked as they shared a healthy laugh and continued to flirt as the food was being prepared.

They discussed watching a few movies and spending time together all weekend long. Also, they even had a few trips planned out over the next few weeks. It was all good, and the day was going pretty good. Nighttime came around, and they had the movie watching them because the movie was not being watched. Those two love birds were so caught up in each other that they didn't hear the disturbing noise that was about to catch them both completely off guard.

Carlos ran with a gang called Real Right Gang or RRG for short. So, with Carlos being missing for almost a month, his team began making revenge plans and had been on a hunt for Carlos. They had no idea if he was alive or if he was dead, but they planned on checking out every clue they could come up with. They had meetings and resources all around town. RRG was popular for selling half of the best smoking weed in town, so they knew who all Carlos, who was one of the gang's top sellers, had business deals with. It didn't take long for someone to mention the time Cee Money called herself running off on Carlos, and he had to teach her ass a lesson about the streets. Them little pretty bitches thought shit was sweet until something sour happened to their asses. So, after Carlos took his money back from her the old school way, she began making all types of threats about what she was going to get done to him.

Therefore, she became one of the three people they were going to kidnap until they got some answers, and tonight, they were two cars deep and about to put the revenge plan into action. The plan didn't involve killing the bitch; they figured she was just the average local city girl who played tough but wasn't really hitting on anything. Besides, the RRG wasn't known for any killing for real. They just felt like they had to get revenge for Carlos. Social media had them gassed up, and they really thought they were some tough guys now because of all the attention they got because of all the money they were making. Money gassed people up. Some even felt like they had to do something dangerous to prove they were not soft. So, the few flunkies that headed toward Cee Money's spot had no real experience. A few were scared, and only one would actually pull the trigger if necessary. The others were just some followers who hid behind their money.

"Who car is that?" one of them in the first car asked as they crept up toward the driveway.

"It don't matter. Whoever inside getting the same treatment! I know this sneaky ass hoe knows what happened to Carlos. Let's get this revenge, my nigga!" The two pairs of cars spilt up. Some went around the back, and some went around the front, so there would be no way out — or so they thought.

Chapter 4

"Yass, Daddy, you like how I work that pussy riding on the tip of that dick? I know you wanna cum all inside this tight, hot pussy. Shit, ohh, this dick feel so good." Cee Money was riding on top of Rednose like a stripper. She was being freakier than usual. She was sweating harder too. Rednose knew she was geeked up on the Percs.

She had been sliding up and down on his dick for over thirty minutes.

The sex was good and made Rednose want to fully submit to the pleasure and just flat out enjoy it. However, he never let his guard down and was always overthinking everything. He had never been to the military, but his father and grandfather were veterans, so he believed it was in his DNA to always stay aware and alert. Combined with getting stabbed up while he was sleeping in prison before, he would never get caught lacking again. That was why he kept weapons all over his spot and Cee Money's spot whether the weapons were sticks, knives, mace, guns, of even brass knuckles. He was prepared for anything. Rednose also had a special gift. It was hard to explain, but he knew when imminent danger was near, and he could see things before they happened. So, before he heard a loud kick, he was already seeing visions of disastrous events about to happen. He would try to shake it off as PTSD from being institutionalized or as paranoia because of his high anxiety levels.

"Baby, what you…" Cee Money was cut off mid-sentence.

"Shut the fuck up. It's a bunch of niggas surrounding your house! I thought nobody knew where you stayed, bitch. You had that nigga over here earlier. You slipping!" Rednose was whispering very aggressively with his hands on her neck.

Cee Money's eyes were big and moving around nervously. You could tell she had a million thoughts running around her brain all at once.

"You heard that?" she asked Rednose, but he didn't respond.

Rednose was moving quickly, and she didn't know whether to follow him or hide underneath the cozy blankets on her queen-sized bed.

Rednose emerged from the darkness with two guns and a long knife. He had just turned all the lights off. He was trying to explain something to Cee Money, but then, a glass shattered. At the same time, the front door was kicked in.

Pop!

Rednose shot the body that was trying to break and enter through the window the glass was shattered in, which was Cee Money's bedroom.

The first question that came to his mind was how in the hell did the person know that was her bedroom. Weird.

"Shit, run!" was all Rednose heard from the window. That was when he realized there was more than one subject trying to get through the window because the target he hit went down immediately. The others scattered and slowly regrouped.

Rednose heard Cee Money screaming as two figures appeared and tried to grab at her small frame. She tried to fight back but was taken down. When the figures saw Rednose, it was too late. Rednose was able to stab the first guy several times and take him out instantly. All the prison knife fights had Rednose very skilled with knives. That was why he preferred to use them instead of guns. The other guy was aiming at Rednose, trying to get a shot off. It was too dark, and Rednose was moving so low and fast on the ground that it was difficult. That was when Cee Money picked up one of the small handguns Rednose had out and started shooting at the figure aiming at Rednose. It took her four or five shots, but she was finally able to hit him once in the arm, causing him to drop his weapon and flee.

"Stay low, baby. Don't move. Stay low," Rednose whispered to Cee Money as he ran to the window and checked, but there was nobody trying to get in. Next, he looked at the body of the victim he stabbed up. He was bleeding so badly from the stab wounds that he was slipping out of consciousness. The plush, white, fluffy carpet in Cee Money's bedroom was now soaked in dark red blood. The other figure had managed to stumble back out the front door and had disappeared. Rednose paused to gather his thoughts for a few minutes. He saw Cee Money shaking and throwing up over by her bed. Her eyes were big because of shock. The guy looked dead to her, but Rednose knew he wasn't. The sound of cars speeding away from the area gave Rednose the confidence that the resistance him and Cee Money put up had run off the robbers.

To make sure, Rednose checked out the outside of the house and the back by the window. The only thing that was there was spots of blood and broken glass from the window. That was when he heard the police cars from a distance. He raced back inside and grabbed all his things.

"Baby, come on. Let's go. We gotta get the fuck outta here now. We going to my spot. Don't pack nothing. Just come on." Rednose was picking her up and grabbing her by the arm. Cee Money was attempting to go get something, but Rednose refused and forced her into his car, and they disappeared before the cops came. Right before they left, Cee Money nearly tripped over the body that was bleeding on her plush, white carpet. She happened to look down at the body. The man was wearing a Pooh Shiesty ski mask, but she still saw the tattoo on his neck, and it instantly sent chills all through her body.

"How the fuck them niggas knew where you stayed?" Rednose immediately snapped after they made it out the neighborhood and got on the expressway headed to Columbus, Georgia.

Cee Money just sat quietly and stared straight ahead. Rednose was getting snake vibes. Even though her vibe was weird for some odd reason, Cee Money was not the reason for the attack. Rednose was the reason Carlos was missing, and Cee Money didn't know anything about that. Rednose didn't know the guys were coming to get revenge for Carlos because he was under the impression that nobody from Columbus knew where she lived.

"I'm going to jail," Cee Money said after a long period of silence in the car. Rednose didn't respond. He just took all the back roads and avoided traffic as much as possible until he was at his spot. He got out the car with Cee Money and went inside his spot. His one-bedroom duplex was located on the north side of Columbus, Georgia. It was way out of the way of all the action and drug dealings going on around the gutter parts of the city. Nobody even knew he was out, but he still kept a very low profile and chose to live in a remote area. He had a lot of his money still in accounts, but he also had a nice bankroll put up in his spot that not even Cee Money knew about.

Rednose hopped in the shower to clean up. He had blood all over himself, but it was not his blood. He put the bloody clothes in a black trash bag after he got out of the shower. He went out of his back door and set the bag of clothes on fire and lit a blunt he had put out earlier. He took deep pulls as he watched the fire devour the bag instantly. He was in deep thought and zoned out in a meditative stage without even realizing it. The whole ordeal replayed in his head over and over. He was now able to count.

There were at least four people. He counted two at the window and two on the inside. Those guys knew exactly how to get inside and exactly which window was Cee Money's bedroom.

"This bitch got some explaining to do for real," he said to himself as he took one more puff then flicked the roach of the blunt in the air and watched it fall by the ashes he'd just created. "Buddy might not make it," he said without thinking, referring to the guy he stabbed up to protect himself and Cee Money. Shoot first, ask questions later. Now it was time for the questions.

When Rednose came back inside, he saw that Cee Money's head was buried in her phone, but she put it down instantly when she saw him. She sat her phone down and folded her arms and stared at Rednose as if she had something on her mind.

"Rednose, where is Carlos?" she flat out asked him. This surprised the hell out of Rednose.

"Who is that?" Rednose fired back at her, playing stupid. This gave him time to think about this. Why was she asking about Carlos? And how come every time he was about to question her, she found a way to distract him? Rednose walked up to Cee Money and tried to grab her phone. She snatched it away quickly like it was a basketball and she was a professional point guard.

"Give me your phone!" he demanded.

"Nigga, no!" she replied.

"Bitch, give me the muthafucking phone!" he yelled.

"Who the fuck you calling a bitch?" Now she was pissed.

They continued to wrestle for the phone a few more minutes until he had her pinned down with her arms above her head. She tried to buck and was kicking her legs, so he used his knees to stop all movement. She couldn't do anything now.

So, he bent her wrist. She screamed like somebody was trying to take her virginity. You know how those females overreacted. Finally, she dropped the cell phone.

"Ouch, man, you just broke my wrist!" she cried while holding her wrist with her other hand.

Rednose knew she was faking because he didn't even put that much pressure on it.

"What's the lock code?" he asked her several times, but she just kept crying about her wrist being broken.

"You did something to Carlos. That's why them RRG niggas broke in my house and tried to kill me! Nigga, now the police and news people at my house, looking for me like I'm some kind of killer! I hate you! Take me to my mom's house now!"

Chapter 5

After a few hours of conversation, Rednose and Cee Money felt like they didn't even know each other. Rednose knew she wasn't being totally truthful with him and kept hiding certain things. Cee Money felt like Rednose was a psychopath with a dark side that was very dangerous. He still didn't attempt to share or reveal any information about Carlos. He also didn't confirm if Carlos was dead or alive. However, Cee Money did advise Rednose that she recognized a tattoo on the intruder's neck that read, "RRG." That indicated the home invasion was in retaliation for Carlos. But she still didn't know how she became a target. With Rednose not telling her much information, she became furious and fearful.

"I can't go back home, and them niggas know exactly where my sister stays at, bra. You need to tap in with RRG and tell them niggas I didn't have shit to do with anything. My family in danger now, and you just killed a nigga in my fuckin home! My bedroom!" Cee Money started crying again, pacing back-and-forth nervously.

"What you saying? Huh?" Rednose asked her, standing up, getting all in her face. He was tired of the snake vibes and knew the bitch was on the verge of flipping the script. Hoes like that were the type to come to court and get on the stand and testify against you. She still didn't explain how the RRG members knew where she stayed because that would expose who she really was, and that wasn't part of her plan.

Cee Money was definitely money hungry, and that was the vibes she'd been giving since day one. Rednose was so impressed by the way she held him down that he dismissed her greedy ways. But now, she was acting weird. Not to mention, she was the reason he took the Carlos situation so personally, which clouded his judgement and clear thinking. He never thought about the fact that this bitch was probably fucking Carlos on the low.

"How did them RRG members know your personal location?" Rednose asked, breaking the silence. He sat back down and folded his arms while looking her directly in the eyes.

"I don't know," she answered in a low voice. Her eyes said she was lying because she couldn't keep eye contact. But Rednose didn't know for sure. He knew this bitch was his weakness, but he hoped he was wrong. "We need to go check on my sister, and what am I supposed to tell the police?" Cee Money got the pressure off of her by changing the subject like most females did when they were hiding something. They played victim and helpless. "My sister." She said it so sad that it made Rednose want to go help her.

"You don't tell the police shit! You still got your lawyer, correct?" he asked, knowing she did have a lawyer.

"Yes, should I call him?" Cee Money responded like an innocent child.

"Yeah. Tell him something happened at your address, and you are laying low until you speak to him. Don't mention nothing else and don't say nothing about anything. Don't reveal no unnecessary information. Now, how do these niggas know where your sister stay?" Rednose was definitely on her ass, not letting anything get past without investigation.

"Because she used to fuck with RRG Ray." Cee Money explained how they met and how they fell out after Cee Money and her sister jumped on RRG Ray's baby mama. All Rednose could think was that this was some ghetto ass, ratchet, hood rat type shit going on. When Cee Money told the story, she would get all into it, just like a city girl.

"So, that explains how they knew where you stayed," Rednose said out loud, trying to put the details together.

"Hell no! I don't fuck with them niggas!" Cee Money responded defensively. "Let me call my sister. I got a feeling something not right." Cee Money called her sister. No answer. She called again. No answer. Next, she texted her.

Rednose was just looking at her and thinking he should have never gone after Carlos for this bitch because she was showing another side of her that he never knew even existed. But he was in love with her, so he didn't know how to feel for real. All this was new to him. The way she twirled on his dick and bussed that pussy open anytime he wanted it had him feeling some type of way. So, he had conflicting emotions toward her.

They jumped in his car and drove toward Cee Money's sister's house. The whole time they drove, Cee Money kept calling her sister's cell phone but wasn't getting any response. She was nervous and had a bad feeling about the situation. She couldn't believe Rednose actually came home from prison and went after Carlos. Even though he refused to admit it, it was the only explanation. She remembered him going on and on about how he was going to handle Carlos the first days he came home. Now, all this drama going on had her feeling crazy and angry.

"Toria, open the door, bitch," Cee Money yelled as she knocked on the door for several minutes. Rednose just sat in the driver's seat, rolling up a blunt.

Rednose began to think about the events that had taken place after he kidnapped Carlos from the bowling alley. The things he did to that boy sent chills up his arms, so he was trying to think about something else when, suddenly, Cee Money came back to the car and opened the passenger's door.

"Something ain't right. My sister not answering nor is she home," Cee Money complained as she dropped her fat booty on the seat and tried to call again. No answer.

"Did you try to open the door? It looks unlocked," Rednose said with the blunt in his mouth, about to fire it up.

At that moment, Cee Money paid attention to the door and noticed it was in fact unlocked. She ran back to the front door and opened it before Rednose could say anything else. He knew things may not be good, so he was out the car with a gun in his hand before she started screaming.

Rednose didn't know what Cee Money saw, but judging from the way she screamed, it had to be a dead body. He followed the sound of her crying and went upstairs into a bedroom. The room looked like a fight had taken place, and there were bloody puddles on the carpet. Cee Money was crying and shaking badly.

"This shit your fault!" she yelled and began swinging wild punches at Rednose that he easily avoided, only getting hit in his chest and arms.

"Baby, please calm down. It might not be what it looks like. Let's check the rest of the house to see if she in here somewhere passed out. Come on. Hurry up." Rednose finally got her to calm down enough to talk sense in her.

They searched the rest of the spot, but nobody was there. Cee Money broke down crying again, so Rednose had to damn near carry her back to the car. Once inside the car, she started kicking and screaming viciously. She even tried to jump out the car again, but Rednose locked the car doors.

"Baby, calm the fuck down and listen so I can think! Damn, now is not the time to panic. We have to figure this out with our head clear, okay?" Rednose saw Cee Money trying to get it together when, suddenly, her iPhone started vibrating. It was her sister.

"Hello... Toria?"

"No, bitch, this ain't yo slut ass sister," the voice replied.

"Who the fuck is this, and where is my sister?" Cee Money asked fearfully.

Rednose sat quietly and focused on the voice he could hear because the car was so silent.

"We got your sister, bitch, and we about to cut this hoe throat unless you tell us what we need to know and don't play with it. All you have to do is tell us the truth, and it will set your freaky ass sister free. Now, where is RRG Los?" The voice was talking slow but demanding.

Cee Money knew RRG Los was, in fact, Carlos, and this made her throw a quick, evil look at Rednose before she answered. "Man, I swear my hand to God I don't know nothing about that shit y'all got going on with Carlos, but if y'all don't bring my sister home, I'ma call the police!"

At that moment, Cee Money knew she had fucked up. She heard her sister screaming in the background, and some laugher followed behind that.

"China, please help me! Just tell them what they want. I can't leave my daughter. She needs me. Please, Cee!" was all she heard her sister say before someone took the phone away from her face.

"Listen, Caria, aka Cee Money, or whatever your pussy selling ass go by these days, these niggas over here drinking, and you know how them boys get when they drunk. I'm sure you remember. Yeah, you know what's going on. Toria's ass going to start looking all phat, and niggas going to get horny. So, you got a few hours before your sister gets ran through. After we slut the bitch out, you know I can't let her live anymore, so you need to go figure out something. I'll be in touch soon." The caller disconnected.

Cee Money just stared at the phone before she broke down crying again. This was too much for her to bear. Yeah, she had been outside in the streets since she was in middle school, but she never experienced anything like this at all. She knew that her sister could get raped, and it brought back memories of all the nights she was taken advantage of. She cried harder, knowing Rednose had heard the allegations about her selling pussy, and he would definitely find out about her past now.

It was only a matter of time. She could feel his energy change and knew he had heard everything. He was in deep thought, and that worried her, especially because her sister was in a very dangerous situation.

Meanwhile, Rednose was putting all kinds of things together in his head, like the fact that the man said Cee Money sold pussy and how she claimed she recognized a tattoo and knew the RRG members were responsible for breaking and entering into her spot. How did those niggas even know where Cee Money and her sister lived? Yeah, the snake vibes were different there, and he knew Cee Money had another life that he hadn't been made aware of.

"Oh, my goodness, what am I going to do?" Cee Money broke the silence in a low voice full of genuine fear. She was absolutely scared to death. Those RRG members were known for getting money and pimping type shit. She never thought they were some kidnapping, raping murderers. She looked at Rednose and put her head on his strong chest and cried harder.

Rednose reluctantly put his hands around her to make her feel safe, but he wasn't feeling her the same anymore. Everything about her felt sneaky and weird. The way she worked her pussy, he should have known this bitch was a professional whore. He couldn't believe she was sitting here crying and acting like that man didn't just put her on blast for selling pussy. She didn't even defend herself or try to explain anything. This had Rednose so angry that he zoned out and was just feeling regret. However, he still had serious love for her. Maybe if she told the truth from the start, it could have been different, but the sneaky, snake shit had him blown.

He hated sneaky, lying, conniving bitches.

They drove back to Rednose's spot in silence. They were both deep in thought. Once inside, Cee Money had a mood swing and started yelling and screaming at him about everything being his fault. She said she wished she'd never met him. She kept attacking Rednose, but after a while, she broke down and started begging Rednose for help. When he asked her what the caller knew about her and if she was a former prostitute, she denied it but said she used to tease niggas and get money from them all the time. She said RRG used to be real tricks and would pay her bills, but she claimed she never had sex with any of the members but used to just flirt and finesse them out of money. Rednose knew she was a good liar, so he asked her again how the RRG members knew where she stayed at. She continued to claim she didn't know. They went in circles until Rednose realized she wasn't switching up her story, so he let it go.

"So, where is Carlos, and don't keep lying because nobody never tried Carlos until you came home. Remember you told me you was going to get at him for robbing me. So, did you kill him? Are you holding him hostage somewhere, you crazy motherfucker?" Cee Money was getting hyped up with each word she spoke.

"I told you I ain't do shit to buddy! Why you keep asking me about that fuck nigga? Let's just go to all them niggas' spot and I'll snatch one of they ass up and torture him until he contacts the rest. Once we get him begging for mercy, we will get the drop on your sister, then I'll go rescue her and take all them niggas' money. I'll kill each and every last one of them. Matter of fact, I'll make them fuck niggas show me where they holding all the money and drugs at and take that too. I'll put a end to they whole little gang. How about that?"

Cee Money knew this nigga was crazy as fuck and was dead ass serious. She knew the RRG members were too deep for a one-man army. She knew more about them than she told Rednose. Her sister didn't have much time left, so she had to come up with a plan, and she needed to do it quickly.

"Okay, Rednose. Baby, you right. We gotta send a blitz at them, and I know where my sister ex lives at, but can you take me to my mom's house first? I need to get myself together and go come up with a good story, so she don't call the police. You feel me?" Cee Money wrapped her arms around Rednose and told him her plan, and he was all ears.

"Okay, baby, you don't wanna wait till the sun comes up? You don't think popping up like this going to look weird to your moms?" Rednose asked with genuine concern. He kissed her forehead as he saw her in deep thought.

"You kinda right, but fuck all that. My sister life is in danger right now, not later! I have to go home and get my tablet with my old phone password. That's the only way I can dig up his address. You feel me?" Cee Money said, "You feel me?" the same way Rednose said it, so he could understand her situation.

"Okay, baby. Fuck it. Let's go." Rednose reluctantly agreed but hoped she didn't get with her mother and call the cops because he would probably get his name dropped in that. He loved Cee Money, but he would slice that bitch's throat before he went back to prison.

They drove for what seemed like forever to the south side of town. Rednose never thought he would be back on this side right now, especially after the situation with Mook and the shootout at the store a few weeks ago. He was keeping up with Mook and was sure he was still locked up, but he didn't know when he would get released.

Also, the female shooter most definitely got a good look at him, so he knew he would have to push her wig back if he ever came across her again. He figured Mook didn't know he was out, but Mook did know his voice and the way he looked, even with a mask on. So, he needed to handle his situation with those weak ass RRG members, so he could finish Mook off for good this time. Once those two situations were handled, he could start taking out some of his main targets. After that, him and Cee Money could get the fuck out of the city and head for the West Coast. Seven was the number of targets he had to take out according to his plan. Four out of the seven were going to stuff his bags up with enough cash to start his business up in California. He would reveal everything to Cee Money once the plan was complete, and they were settled on the West Coast popping champagne.

"What you doing, baby?" Rednose asked, glancing in her direction.

"Oh, nothing. Just texting my mom, telling her to unlock the door for me." Cee Money put her phone up and pointed to the street Rednose needed to merge on in order to reach her mother's house.

"Okay, I'ma call you in a few hours, baby." Cee Money kissed Rednose then got out of the car. He watched her ass jiggle as she jogged up to the front door.

Rednose waited until she was inside before he pulled off and headed back to his spot. He made a phone call as he rode home. Once he got off the phone, he felt like something weird was going on but dismissed the feeling. He made it home, laid across his couch, and turned his flat screen to ESPN and caught up on the highlights. LeBron James was still his goat, but he was impressed with all the young talent in the NBA these days.

Rednose didn't know how long he had been asleep. It could not have been more than a hour and a half, but Cee Money was blowing his phone up.

"Hello. What's up? I had fell asleep. I'm sorry," Rednose admitted.

"Baby, wake up. Come pick me up. I'm at my cousin's apartment, and we just got the drop on my sister ex-boyfriend. I got his exact location right now." Cee Money was talking fast and excited.

"Your cousin apartment? Baby, how you get from your mother house to your cousin apartment?" Rednose stood up and grabbed his two handguns and a bag of items before he locked up his place.

"Because them niggas called me back and was saying they was going to rape my sister if I didn't tell them something, so I called my cousin, and he picked me up, but now, I need you to come pull up on me asap, so we can go get at this nigga before daylight," Cee Money explained.

"Okay, okay, baby. I'm on my way. Just tell me how to get there." Rednose was already on the expressway, headed toward the other side of town.

He stayed on the phone with her as she gave him directions. While he was on the phone with Cee Money, he sent a text message out.

"I'm outside on the porch. The light on. It's a one way in, one way out, short street, baby. Hold up! You just passed the street. I just saw your car. Turn around and come on the street you just passed." Cee MONEY was telling Rednose how to get to her.

Rednose turned on another street that was next to it and made a U-turn and got back on the main street. When he turned on the street Cee Money said she was on, another car turned in behind him. He glanced in the rearview mirror but didn't pay too much attention to it.

"Right here, park right there. Okay, baby. I love you, and I'm sorry for everything," Cee Money said then hung up.

"Sorry for everything? The fuck you talking about?" Rednose said to the phone, but she was gone.

All of a sudden, the car that was behind his stopped a few cars away from him, and two shooters hopped out, but Rednose saw them first. Then, something else caught his attention. Two more niggas were running down on each side of his car from the two apartment buildings. He was caught in a triangle ambush. Cee Money had double crossed him. It was a set up. Stanky, sneaky, no-good bitch!

Chapter 6

Imagine being in the middle of a triangle, surrounded by shooters. You could either panic then become a sitting duck, or you could drop your nuts and shoot your way out of the jam. Rednose didn't have time to think. He'd been in a few shootouts before he went to prison. He was shot a couple of times, but none were life threatening. In prison, he'd been in a bunch of knife fights. He almost lost his life once before after being caught in a jam. That time, he'd panicked. Afterwards, he told himself that he would never fold up when being attacked by a group. In fact, the next time he got ambushed and was caught up in a jam, he would rush the crowd and catch them off guard. That was exactly what he did.

First, Rednose did a quick observation of his total surroundings. There was one car behind him with shooters, a shooter on foot coming from the left, and another shooter creeping from the right. He could tell they didn't know what they were doing, but it looked good if they were trying to scare somebody. The closest shooter was the one coming from the left, the same side where Cee Money was supposed to have been on a porch. Rednose hopped out, stayed low, and fired at the shooter, catching him completely off guard. He tried to run but was hit and dropped his weapon before he stumbled on the grass. Rednose ran low and fast away from the car and other shooter. He was shooting behind his back as he ran. Rednose was moving like a professional assassin. If these streets punks were smart or had any skills, they would have not let him get out the vehicle and scatter around the darkness like that. Now, it was hard to hit him. A few people that were outside were now running in all directions, which made it harder to get Rednose.

The shooter that was on foot met up with the shooter that got out of the car, and they were now standing over the shooter that Rednose shot down. Rednose saw this interaction going on from the dumpster he was hiding behind. From reading the body language, the guy he hit was probably still alive. He saw another man come out with a gun to a female's head then lead her to a car. Next, two of the shooters picked up their mans and carried him to a car that had just pulled up and put him inside. The car sped away as quickly as it pulled up. At that moment, Rednose knew he was dealing with a large group of people that pretty much had these apartments as a main base. You could tell everyone in this apartment complex ran with these guys. Rednose knew he had to get the hell out of there, or he was going to become a sitting duck. He wasn't even happy about not getting shot. All he could think about was how Cee Money set him up and sold him out like that. This had a burning feeling in his chest. It was like a part of him was hurting badly. He was filled with rage, and his heart was broken all in one.

His phone began to vibrate, which brought him out of the trance he had slid into. It was a private number, so he ignored it.

"Where the fuck she at?" he asked himself, thinking about the Plan B he had put together because he knew something wasn't right with Cee Money. He just had to actually see it to believe it, and it nearly cost him his life force. Just then, his phone rang again, and it was his backup plan.

"Yeah, meet me at the Churches across from the apartments. Okay, you already there? Good, I knew I could count on you. Yes, I'm okay. You was right about that dog ass hoe. I'ma take care of her personally, but Carlos' family and them RRG niggas finna hurt real bad after my next act. The show just getting started."

Rednose disconnected the call and checked to make sure the coast was clear before he made a dash for the wooded area. He jumped a fence and landed hard on something. "Aggggghhhh, fuck!" he yelled, falling on his ass in agony. He grabbed his left ankle. He knew he had broken it or something because it swelled up instantly. He must have been making noise because he heard a few junkies coming toward him. Next, he heard a dog barking. Those two factors made him briefly ignore the pain. He ran like hell until he was across the street from the apartments. Then, he walked in pain up a dark street until he came behind the Churches' building. He saw her car at about the same time as he heard a group of niggas running toward him.

"There his bitch ass go right there! Shoot him!" a voice yelled before shots rang out.

Rednose sent shots back to buy more time. The shooters didn't stop their pursuit. They just ducked down when he shot back. Fortunately, Rednose was able to jump inside the getaway car before the shooters were anywhere near hitting him. As they drove away, one bullet hit the back bumper but didn't cause any real damage. It only made the driver's survival skills kick in, and she got them to safety.

"You good, boo?" the light-skinned girl with the long, reddish colored dreadlocks asked him as she got on the interstate.

"Yeah, take me to my spot so I can pack all my shit. That bitch knows where I stay. I'm moving out," Rednose reluctantly stated. You could hear defeat in his voice.

The female driver noticed that also. She saw the sadness and shame all over his face. While he was usually joyful and confident, at the moment, he looked very weak and confused.

The female's name was Ebony, and she was Rednose's female friend.

They'd been cool for a while, even before he went to prison. She wasn't into girls back then, and he remembered her very well. Nowadays, she was more of the tomboy type. She wore men clothes, but Rednose knew she had a banging body she was hiding. She was the quiet and submissive type, totally the opposite of Cee Money's wild, unstable ass. Rednose kept her out of his personal business, but she did know about the young girl he was dating, and she hadn't approved since day one. When she tried to put Rednose on game about her past and reputation in the city, Rednose stopped her and said he did not want to hear it because it had nothing to do with him and would make him look at her differently. All he knew was nobody was perfect, and she had helped him get out of prison, and that alone got her in his heart. But now, he wished he would have listened to Ebony when he first got out. Her advice was to keep Cee Money as just a girl he got money with and had sex with from time to time but not to fall in love or trust her because she was a dog. So, that was the reason Rednose made that call to Ebony before he went to meet Cee Money at the apartments, and he texted her and told her that he needed her to be posted across from the apartments at the Churches because his guts told him Cee Money was either calling the police or was going to try and swap him out for her sister. He put it together in his head without saying anything at all. The phone call from the RRG member said it all. It gave Rednose a vision in his head that both Cee Money and her sister, Toria, had some ties with RRG whether they used to fuck them for money or set up niggas for them. And Rednose felt like Carlos was either Cee Money's ex-boyfriend or a nigga who used to pimp her. Carlos was in his forties, and the other members were younger.

So, maybe he was the plug or the leader of the group. That was what made Rednose not even say anything about Carlos after the way Cee Money was acting when the members broke in her apartment. So many mysterious activities had happened in sequence. How did they know where she stayed? Where her bedroom window was? Her phone number? Her sister's address? And what made them think she had something to do with Carlos' disappearance? Did she post something crazy or troll them? Did she say something to someone who said something to someone else? Once they got her sister and she said drop her off, Rednose knew immediately she was planning on double crossing him. Nothing beat the double but the triple cross. That was how he was able to see the shooters before they were about to shoot and how he was able to have a getaway driver on standby. Now, he was about to make Carlos go viral.

First, he had to call the police and report his car stolen. Next, he got all his things from his spot and packed it up and put it inside Ebony's car. He had Ebony hold his other gun as they kept watch in case Cee Money had already sent them RRG members to his spot. The sun was coming up now, but that didn't mean anything in the city these days. So many home invasions took place in broad daylight that it was insane. Afterwards, they went to Ebony's spot and had a long, deep conversation. Now, there was a backup plan put together, and Cee Money and the RRG gang was about to become ghosts. They'd just unlocked Rednose, the monster.

Chapter 7

Rednose drove his new car to a restaurant on the north side of town with Ebony on the passenger side. They had been spending a lot of time together and did some wild things as a duo. He didn't know she was a lowkey goon. The way she performed during some of the missions they went on showed Rednose he wasn't dealing with a little girl nor a rookie. This level of skills only came with experience. Rednose and Ebony now had some more money after they took out a few of the RRG members and also one of the guys Rednose had on his original list of targets.

He had sent Ebony to distract him as he cleared out his spot, and they split the money up. There was no argument or petty debates. She was quiet and very helpful. She never questioned his knowledge or information like Cee Money's nosy ass used to do. Speaking of Cee Money, she was going to get what was coming to her real soon. Rednose had not heard from her at all since the night she tried to double cross him. She was obviously laying low. He wasn't sure if she had contacted the police after her house was invaded or what. He wasn't even sure if the guy he had stabbed up was still alive or had bled out on her bedroom floor. He did not care to wonder if her sister was safe or not. All that went out the window with his feelings when reality hit. She actually tried to set him up and left him for dead. How could a female go from helping a man run up some lawyer money and getting him out of prison, laying up with him every night and planning on spending your life with him, starting a new life with him, moving across the country with him, to being mad at him for getting revenge on a guy that supposedly robbed you and then setting him up to get kidnapped and possibly killed?

After analyzing the situation with a clear head, Rednose was absolutely sure Cee Money still had feelings for Carlos and was not loyal at all to anyone but her money hungry ways. Also, after long talks with Ebony, he learned more information about RRG. They were the talk of the city and had the most money in the streets, and Carlos was the top dawg. These guys weren't known to be real killers. They just had a lot of fake clout and made it look good and dangerous. Truth be told, they just used their money and influence to manipulate young girls and build their reputation up. They should have never come for Rednose because now, he wasn't going to show them any mercy.

He cancelled all of his old plans and was focused on the entire scoop of RRG. He spent hours stalking all of their social media accounts and keeping taps of their whereabouts. With Ebony and her younger brother, Coby, on his side, they formed their own gang called "RRG Killers."

Coby and Ebony were already robbing and stealing cars before Rednose got out of prison. So, now with him, they were a dangerous combination. Rednose decided to upgrade lil Coby to a good shooter. They would hit the shooting range on the weekends after Rednose's weekly gym routine. Ebony refused to be left out, so she would come as well. She surprised Rednose with her shooting skills. After he asked her how she learned how to shoot, she shared a deep story with him.

"The first time I ever had sex was when I was in high school. My boyfriend burned me with a STD. Then, when I asked him about it, he acted like I was cheating on him and must of got it from someone else because he didn't have it.

That shit pissed me off so bad because he was the only person I gave my body to.

"Like this nigga took my innocence, and I can't never get that back. So, one day, I laid in his bushes and hopped out on him and robbed him," she said while shooting at the target. They were at the shooting range when she told the story.

"Wait, so you actually laid in his bushes and hopped out on him like a Tubi TV movie?" Rednose asked, laughing, but he saw she wasn't smiling.

"Hell yeah, nigga. I wore layers of clothes and shit with a mask on. He thought I was a dude. I even changed my voice. He was pussy, and I took all his shit!" Ebony confirmed then started back shooting with more rage.

At that moment, Rednose knew she was different from other women. He also learned she hadn't been with a guy sexually since then, only girls.

He also learned that Coby used to date the same female that a RRG member named Ice Water used to date. They called him Ice Water because he was a good shooter. Coby and Ice Water had gotten into a fight over the female. Ice Water could not respect that Coby got the best of him, so his hoe ass ran and told his RRG members. They jumped on Coby and put the video on the internet to add to his humiliation. A few months later, Ice Water was coming to pick up the same girl and caught her and Coby kissing. That was when he shot at them, hitting Coby once in the arm but killing the girl instantly. Ice Water was never charged with the body. However, he had gotten arrested for another assault for shooting someone else. It was no wonder they called him Ice Water; the nigga didn't miss! He was supposed to be getting out in a few more months, and Coby wanted to step on him. That was when Rednose decided to form the gang, RRG Killers.

There was only three of them, but they were vicious and had personal motivation.

Another thing that helped them out was that Ebony had military experience, and her father was in the service currently. He had a spot on base in Fort Benning, Georgia. Also, her grandma was retired with a bunch of weapons in her basement that Ebony and Coby had access to. There were enough in there to take down an entire neighborhood.

"Yes, can I get a cobb salad and a number three?" Ebony said to the lady on the drive thru intercom. Rednose was smoking a blunt, vibing to the low playing J. Cole music in the background.

After Ebony ordered the food, Rednose looked at his phone and saw it was ringing. He let the call go to voicemail. He needed time to gather his thoughts, so he just stared at the phone in disbelief. He couldn't believe Cee Money had the balls to call him. What did she think she was about to do, troll him? The fact that she even called him like he wasn't going to put a bullet through her skull was insane to him.

"Tobias! You going to pull off or what?" Ebony asked him, calling him by his real name.

"Yeah, my bad. Let's go." Rednose passed her the hot food bags then drove off with the music still down.

He half expected his phone to ring again, and it didn't. Well, not until they got back inside Ebony's spot where Coby was playing *Call of Duty* on the game system. He was an all-day gamer for sure, but Rednose was trying to see what type of games this dirty dog ass hoe was playing.

"Where you at?" was how Rednose answered the call.

"Rednose, listen to me. I know you are upset right now, but they made me do it. They told me if I didn't call you to come to the apartments, they was going to kill me and my sister. I know you don't got shit to say to me, but I have to show you something, and after you get this picture, please call me back." Cee Money disconnected. She had the innocent voice down pat.

A few minutes later, Rednose got a picture message. "What the fuck?" was all he could say.

Coby saw the look of confusion all over Rednose's face, so he jumped up to go look at what had his big homie upset. "Oh, shit, you got somebody pregnant, my nigga?" Coby said, looking at the pregnancy test in the picture.

Rednose reluctantly dropped his head and was quiet for a few minutes.

"What's going on in here? What are y'all talking about?" Ebony came out the kitchen where she was eating her food. Rednose passed her the phone, and she saw the picture. She blinked twice then did a double take. She burst out laughing and passed the phone back to Rednose.

"That hoe is money hungry as hell. Wow, she really is trifling, real bad. If you call her back, I bet she ask you for the money for an abortion. That test result shit is a scam. It's fake, brother. They sell them online. When I finish eating, I'm going to show you the exact website she got that shit from. That girl is a professional assassin. She eat niggas for breakfast." Ebony was disgusted at this point and walked away.

Rednose just shook his head and decided to play it out when she called back. To come up with a defensive strategy, he needed to know how the offense planned to attack him. So, when Cee Money called back, he was quiet and even acted with a little emotion, just to make her think he was serious and believed the bull crap she was coming up with. She claimed that she was robbed, yet again, but a RRG member had kidnapped her and held her in an abandoned apartment, duct taped and bound, for a few days. After the food ran out, she was able to escape and had been laying low since. She noticed how sick she had become. That was when she decided to take a pregnancy test.

She said she was sure it was Rednose's baby because she had not had sex with anyone else since he'd come home from prison. She made her story sound very believable. She also mentioned her sister was in the abandoned apartment with her, so she rescued her as well before they escaped the apartment and ran for help. She also let Rednose know the guy he stabbed up that had passed out on her plush, white carpet had survived but was arrested for home invasion. If Rednose was not street smart and didn't have Ebony helping him with the loopholes, Cee Money would have had him fooled. She could fool anyone. Her mother, or whoever trained this bitch, taught her how to manipulate and deceive very well. After hearing her explain things for over an hour, Rednose told her he needed time to gather his thoughts, so he would call her back later.

A few days later, Rednose was by himself on the way to a wooden cabin where he had been holding Carlos hostage. Yes, Carlos was still alive. Rednose had just been torturing him and feeding him the bare minimum to survive. He had him chained up inside a cage, blindfolded, surrounded in darkness. The way he treated him was very cruel and unusual. Rednose was sick in the head, and he knew he needed some professional help from a mental health counselor. At first, he didn't know why he hadn't killed Carlos already. Maybe he was just experimenting with him, or maybe he was really upset Carlos had robbed his queen, Cee Money. Or could it be Rednose was just living out his dark, twisted fantasy? Now this was the day Carlos was about to die in a very horrible way. Rednose wasn't going to show him any mercy.

The worst thing that could have happened was for Cee Money to double cross him with RRG after he only wanted to get revenge for Carlos violating her. Now, there was about to be a big news crew, and it would be breaking news all over the country. Rednose was about to commit a modern-day lynching. But first, he needed answers and information to use against Cee Money, her sister, and all the main characters of RRG who tried to kill him. They really had no idea who they were dealing with.

About two hours later, Rednose had his show almost ready to go. He plugged up Carlos' cell phone inside his car to charge it for the grand finale. There was no power inside the wooden cabin, and no one had lived there in years. Rednose had been torturing Carlos and beating him with a baseball bat with barbed wire wrapped around it. The conversation went somewhat like this.

"What you waiting for? Kill me, man, please! What the fuck? You been had me in this motherfucker for what seems like forever! I miss my family! What did I do to you? Is it money? I got plenty of it! Just take me out of my misery. Please! Who are you?" Carlos had broken his normal silence. The first few weeks Rednose had him in the wooden cabin, he used to beg and cry every day. Then, he went into a new phase of just looking like he'd lost his mind and was just making groaning noises and yelling in pain, but there was not too much begging once he realized his abductor wasn't willing to cooperate. But this time, the beating was way more brutal.

Rednose shocked Carlos when he removed his Pooh Shiesty ski mask and started talking. "You really don't know who I am? So, you don't remember when you robbed Cee Money, and she cried out to me, and you said I was never getting out of prison? How did you even know who I was anyway?"

Rednose was kneeling next to Carlos. Carlos had a long rope tied around his neck, and the chain was wrapped around his waist area. It was connected to the wall inside of a dark room in the back of the wooden cabin.

"What the fuck, man? All this is about Cee Money? Get the fuck outta here! Are you serious? Man, you are fucking nuts! You're crazy as fuck!" Carlos was very afraid now and knew at that moment he would never see his family again. So, he did what was asked of him. He answered all questions and unlocked his phone for Rednose. Surprisingly, Carlos' family had either still been paying his phone bill or he had a yearly contract because the phone was still on. This was perfect for Rednose's grand finale.

Carlos had told Rednose everything without holding back anything. It wasn't a surprise that he revealed that Cee Money was his bitch and had been his hoe for a long time. He used to make her sell pussy and taught her how to hustle and finesse niggas. He admitted that the only reason she was fucking with Rednose was because he had gotten another female pregnant and stopped dealing with Cee Money. He also gave up the location to all the main characters of RRG, and he just hoped Rednose would spare his baby mama and child being that all their information was inside the cell phone.

Rednose made a phone call to Coby to go pick up a $100,000 RRG Cuban link chain and some other valuable items from a studio that Carlos owned. Rednose waited for Coby to meet him somewhere else besides the wooden cabin to pick up the chain. He didn't tell Coby anything that he was doing or where he was going. He just told him to stay near his phone and wait on Carlos to go live from his Instagram account real soon.

When Rednose walked back inside the wooden cabin, he caught Carlos trying to break free from the chains, so he grabbed the bat with the barbed wire wrapped around it that was already bloody from earlier and started beating his legs over and over. When Carlos stopped moving, he tied the thick, long rope back around his neck, and then he unhooked the chain. He pulled out his gun and forced Carlos to his knees. Next, he passed Carlos a piece of notebook paper.

"When I turn the camera flash on, you'll be going live. Read that paper slow and loud. If you don't do it good enough, I'ma bring your child's body next to yours." Rednose stepped back and turned on the camera.

Carlos closed his eyes because the bright light was painful and made his head hurt. He was suffering from a swollen brain and broken bones. He didn't have any choice but to read the paper. At this point, he was just ready to die, so the pain would go away.

"To everyone watching this, I'm warning you to leave the city now. If you are a part of Real Right Guys, a.k.a. RRG, you might as well pay for your funeral arrangements. The worst thing y'all did was try to get her to double cross him. Y'all should of left me for dead. Now, the violent crime spree starts. You are about to witness me get lynched and die in front of the same followers I been flexing on for years, in front of the same young girls I manipulated for years. RRG is over. There is a new gang in town called RRG Killers! A monster is on the loose, and you all should be very afraid…"

POP!

Rednose shot Carlos in his left leg, then he set the phone up so the camera could see him pouring gasoline all over the wooden cabin. Next, he grabbed the rope and wrapped it around his right hand twice before he began to drag Carlos aggressively across the wooden flood.

You could hear Carlos yelling in pain and saying he loved his baby mama and child. Rednose dragged his body all the way out the back and then stopped in front of a large tree. He lit a bottleful of newspapers and gasoline and threw it inside the wooden cabin and watched the flames grow rapidly. As the flames grew, he put the phone inside his pocket. While the live was still recording, you could hear Carlos saying, "Please just shoot me. No! Stop! You're crazy!"

When the phone came back out of Rednose's pocket, he recorded Carlos' body dangling from up on the tree. He had literally hung him. The camera caught the last fight Carlos put up, using his legs to try to swing free and pop the rope, but Rednose was a professional with knots and ropes. Rednose let the live viewers see Carlos take his last breath, then he flashed the camera toward the burning wooden cabin. The last thing he showed was the RRG Cuban link necklace. As Rednose drove away, he could see the flames growing in his rearview mirror. His stomach got weak, and he almost threw up. He knew he would not be able to get any sleep for a few days and would have to go burn sage and talk to the spirits. He would also take a spiritual bath to clean his energy before he went back around anybody. He had to put the demons away.

He was already visualizing the future. He was definitely heartbroken after finding out the truth about Cee Money. She was just using him to get over Carlos. She was a prostitute and money hungry slut. He had went after Carlos for nothing. He was really the third wheel. He'd just gotten out of prison and came home to a unnecessary, toxic situation. He should have stuck to his original plan and never gone after Carlos, especially since Carlos never robbed the bitch for real. He just took back his product that he had given her since she was just smoking it up and not making any money.

So, since she had ruined his plans and was now forcing him in a war against the largest group of people in the city, he was going to make her wish she'd never met him at all. He wasn't going to show her any mercy. Cee Money was going to find out why playing games and being money hungry was so dangerous.

Chapter 8

CNN, Fox News, Fox 5, Fox 54, WTVM, WRBL, and all other major news outlets and internet medias were all over the trending story. It had been seven days, but it was still top news everywhere. The rumor reports got more entertaining each day. The worst thing about it was they had named it a "modern day lynching," so there were people coming to the city from all over the country, protesting and demanding answers.

They wanted to know why Carlos was missing for so long and why there wasn't more investigation into his disappearance. Why did the local police treat his strange kidnapping case like it was nothing but a random street gang murder? The rumors included race play and had civil rights activists involved with the rants and protests. All it took was for a few stories to surface about a Black male hanging from a tree. Nothing else was important anymore to most of the people who had become addicted to this developing case. These types of people were suffering from trauma that came from a history of white on Black violence.

The shocking images were banned from being displayed on the national news stations. The Instagram live broadcast had been removed less then twenty-four hours after the body was discovered. However, the video had already been screen recorded and was trending on small, internet media podcasts.

Carlos was last seen alive, but his family already knew what type of life he was living, so they knew it was a greater chance of him being dead than alive. What they didn't expect was the Instagram live broadcast that would never be forgotten. It was absolutely sick and gruesome. The heartbreak was indescribable, so the family reminded quiet as the story grew more popular.

Meanwhile, the RRG members were completely devastated and very nervous. They didn't expect this type of response from one man. He took insane to a new level with no mercy. Big Quan, the main member supplying the group, had placed a large amount of money on Rednose's head, and he would still pay half of that amount if Rednose was just hit by bullets. Cee Money told them everything she knew about Rednose, and they had done his old spot the same way he did the wooden cabin, burned it down. However, he was not affected by it because he hadn't been there since the night he got away from the ambush when Cee Money had double crossed him. Besides, he was expecting this type of retaliation from them. It also confirmed that Cee Money was all the way on their side now and had no more loyalty to him. She had even stopped calling, pretending to be pregnant. She couldn't call his new phone anyway because she didn't have the number. He kept his old phone on for only a few days after Carlos went viral, just to see who would reach out. As he expected, the threats and the, "I'ma kill you, fuck nigga!" calls came back-to-back. It seemed like the entire city was after him. So, he got rid of that phone.

Everybody in the hood and streets were talking about the RRG Cuban link chain and the new RRG Killers gang. Some were trying to figure out who the members were. The streets knew it wasn't a real, modern day lynching, but they didn't really know all the details. Some thought that Carlos was kidnapped because of all the money he was making and figured he was killed because he didn't cooperate. A lot of people were saying he was held hostage way too long for money, so it had to be something personal or just something sick going on.

Some people believed that Carlos was raped by his abductor after a story broke out about his autopsy revealing foul play in his rectum. No major news outlet confirmed nor denied the rumors. There were too many to address, and the investigation was still going on. Therefore, no information would be released publicly until further notice, and the family would be the first to know all the details.

The Instagram live broadcast was filmed live from Carlos' cell phone, which was left next to his hanging body. It was still recording when the police and ambulance arrived to cut his body down. Carlos' family had to watch the police remove his body from the tree because the camera phone wasn't found until about forty-five minutes after they got to the area. He'd received multiple phone calls from disturbed viewers begging the cops to turn the video off. That was when they found it and immediately shut it down. Columbus, Georgia had never witnessed anything this horrible. The community was demanding answers and reassurance regarding their safety. Rednose had made Carlos a breaking news storyline. All he wanted to do was come home and get his money up. He wanted to go on a money hungry mission and reclaim his spot as the top dawg in the city. He didn't plan on being the modern day lyncher. He didn't see Cee Money being more money hungry and savage than him. Now, it was all about survival and warfare. He was directly involved and had the biggest targets on his head. Would he survive, or would the city get revenge for what happened to Carlos?

Chapter 9

It had been months since the breaking news about the modern-day lynching. Carlos' family and friends were still wearing his face on hats and T-shirts. The streets had been surprisingly quiet. Rednose was watching every day from fake social media accounts. It was still unreal to him how easy it was to find out information these days. These new generation people put all their business and told everything about anything to the social media world. It was so easy to figure out information.

Rednose was about to jump in the streets and get on his *Call of Duty* shit for a few days. Before this beef with RRG, Rednose already had an agenda. He had groups of niggas who left him for dead while he was in prison. Some were the same niggas he used to feed and let sleep in his car with him, niggas he bonded out of jail and paid bills for their mamas and shit. However, when Rednose was doing time, he didn't get anything from those niggas, not even seventy cents for some noodles. Honey buns and soups didn't cost that much. It didn't cost anything to keep it real with ya dawg when he was doing hard time in jail or stuck behind the walls in prison. Rednose remembered one time when he called one of his so-called friends just to check on the nigga.

As soon as the pussy nigga answered the phone, he said, "I don't got no money, brah. My cousin told me you called her and was begging for money and shit, brah. We don't have nothing."

Rednose was livid because that friend had never talked to him like that or even raised his voice at him. Also, for him to answer his phone with the negative attitude was disrespectful. "First of all, boy, my mama used to feed you hot plates out my house when your mama was not feeding you or your fat ass cousin, Candice. So, yeah, I did call her and ask for a Cash App last week. I was hungry, and she said no. I did not beg the bitch, but I'm glad I know that's how she took it. I won't bother her anymore. Matter of fact, I'm about to block her sausage biscuit body ass right now. Moreover, pussy nigga, I was just calling you to check on you. I ain't never asked you for no money because you know my situation and you be watching my stories. Why should I ask a nigga who claims he my day one? I still got love for you, but you also tried to fuck my sister over and over again. Why you wait til I came to prison to do some shit like that? I guess you was too pussy to play like that when I was out. Now since you acting like you grew some nuts and you disrespecting me, talking about I'm begging, I'll see you when I get home."

Rednose remembered what the nigga said before he got off the phone.

"I don't argue with niggas who can't even get in the club. You still waiting outside, fuck nigga! You got a life sentence! You still bringing up shit from the past! Nigga, you washed up!"

That was three years ago, but Rednose had elephant memory. As he drove down the street, he went over all the private investigation he had been doing on his friend, Dominique. Dominique had been working for a solar company and was making good money and traveling all over the country working for different job sites. So, Rednose had to wait on him to come back to the city, and today was the perfect day.

As Dominique washed his rims on his new, shiny sports car, he never noticed the car down the street. Someone was inside of the vehicle and had been on a stakeout like outback. Rednose waited for Dominique to finish washing the car before he called him from a prepaid Trax phone that wasn't in anyone's name, so there would be no way to trace the call using police data. Rednose knew better than that. He had sat in the courtroom and seen the evidence being used against defendants. Every phone call and the cell tower the phone was in always told on the location and call durations. Rednose was very sharp, and it would be hard to convict him if he was ever charged with anything. He was ahead of average street punks. That was how he was able to outsmart Dominique.

Rednose knew the exact route Dominique drove when leaving his house. He would make a left then go down a long hill that had a sharp curve. If you were going over sixty miles per hour down the hill when your car was near the curve, it was mandatory that you used your brakes before turning, or your car would go flying off the road. Dominique didn't even know this was his last day driving, and he would regret not paying attention to his surroundings and driving so recklessly.

"Yeah, who this?" Dominique answered the call as he pulled out his driveway. Rednose got directly behind him. He could see the fat meat on the back of Dominique's black ass neck looking like a pack of bologna. He was a dark-skinned, chubby guy that dressed like a rapper.

"What's up, my boy? You don't remember me? You used to tell everyone that I was your best friend. Damn, man, miss you, D-Mack." Rednose called him the nickname he'd given him when they were young.

"How you get my number, nigga? I ain't got shit for a nigga but a hard time. I heard you been in there saying fuck my dead brother and shit. I should put that money on y'all niggas' head, but I'm not worried about it. Just don't call me and ask for nothing, nigga." Dominique was talking to

Rednose like he was still in prison. This nigga was slipping bad.

"You heard I said fuck your dead brother? Nigga, I don't discuss y'all goofy ass niggas, and put some money on y'all head? Who the fuck is y'all? Anyway, fuck all that. I like this all-red, new Mustang you driving with the shiny ass rims. You shouldn't be driving down the hill so fast, bro. What if your brakes went out on you? Remember you said I couldn't get in the club? Well, if you don't find out how to slow your car down, you might not never see the club again, D-Mack." Rednose did a wicked laugh then disconnected.

Dominique looked in his rearview mirror and saw the car behind him. The driver waved at him then blew the horn before hitting the brakes and making a U-turn. This made him panic. He looked at the speedometer and saw he was going over seventy miles per hour. He hit the brakes, but the pedal went to the floor with ease. At that moment, he knew he had been caught slipping and was about to die. The curve was sharp, so he was going to flip the car. There was no way to avoid it. Minutes later, Dominique's car made a sharp turn and went on two wheels before flipping on its side. It flipped four times, tossing his body around, breaking bones. Next, it went airborne then crashed into a large street pole. The impact killed him instantly. The air bag only did more damage to his face because his body was being tossed all over the driver's seat. He would more than likely have a closed casket funeral service. Once the police did an investigation, it would become a homicide case because they would be able to see the brakes had been removed from the Mustang.

A few days later, Rednose was driving down a street, and something was chasing him. He couldn't see if it was an object or what, but he felt the energy of it attempting to devour him. He looked up and noticed that the sky was red, and the sun was blue. At that moment, he told himself he was just dreaming. At this point, Rednose could basically control his dreams and stop things from unfolding. He developed this ability a few years ago and had mastered it completely. This dream was different than any other and felt real, very real. The streets and surrounding area looked familiar, but he could not tell where he was at. The longer he drove, the smaller the street got until he was forced to drive into a river of dark water. The crash felt real because the water was cold and immediately stiffened his joints. All of a sudden, he felt something in the car with him, so he looked in the backseat and saw Dominique and Carlos staring at him with the face of death. This gave him extra energy to pull himself out of the driver's side window and swim out the sinking vehicle.

He looked back as he was swimming away and saw Dominique and Carlos trying to pull his legs back down, so he could drown with them. It felt like he was moving in slow motion, but he was kicking his legs hard and very fast. Finally, he was able to get away from the figures as he made it to the top of the water. He caught his breath then looked all around. The scene had changed. Now, the sky was blue, and the sun was shining its normal color. The bad news was that there was no landscape anywhere in sight — nothing but water. It looked like he was in the middle of the ocean. Rednose then felt something pull him back underwater. He was going down fast, and the sun was becoming harder to see.

As soon as he was about to drown, something weird happened. All the water disappeared. He realized he was in the middle of the ocean, and the water had flat out vanished. Now, he was falling to the endless bottom of the ocean. It felt like he was falling forever. Normally when he had a near death encounter within a dream, he would wake up before he died. This dream was different because every time he was about to die, he would go to a harsher death. Right before he hit the bottom of the ocean, all the gravity stopped working, so he didn't crash on the ocean floor. He just started floating around. He floated around and around for what seemed like forever. There was nothing around him and no one or any type of movement at all. It was the scariest thing he'd ever seen.

"Rednose, wake up, nigga," Coby said, bringing Rednose back to reality. It took him a few seconds to remember where he was, but he was so relieved it was only a dream.

"Boy, where you get that weed from, Coby? Shit had me dreaming about all kind of weird ass shit." Rednose was laughing, but Coby wasn't.

"Tighten up, big brah. These niggas just called me, talking about they finna pull up and shoot the spot up. Word on the street is we had something to do with Carlos' death," Coby announced then went and got his gun.

Chapter 10

As soon as Coby's words settled in, Rednose immediately got up and grabbed his guns. There was no time to ask Coby how word had gotten out about him having something to do with Carlos' death. Rednose walked over to the window and saw three cars creeping down the street.

"Shit, turn off all the lights and get down." Rednose went over to Ebony and snatched her down immediately. As soon as he did, there was a bullet hole put through the wall behind her head.

Ta-tatata-ta-ta-ta-tatata-ta-ta!

Automatic gun shots shattered the windows and ripped through the wallpaper and sheetrock.

"Is everyone good? Coby, Ebony, you okay?" Rednose yelled out after the shots stopped and the cars sped off up the street. Sheetrock was knocked out the wall, big chucks too, but everyone was okay. No one was hit. Ebony was shaken up and still in a kneeling position. Coby was up and racing to go get his Draco. It took Rednose a few minutes to calm Ebony down; she was crying and pretty much terrified. He slowly processed what had just happened. RRG had just got the drop on him.

"Them bitch ass niggas shot up the spot, man. That fuck nigga, Ice Water, just got out. I knew he was going to try to slide, big bra!" Coby was yelling.

"So, you talk to him, nigga?" Rednose's wheels were turning, and he was putting two and two together. Coby must have had some type of argument with Ice Water. Those two were beefing, and it was very serious. The girl they were both in love with was now dead because of Ice Water. So, Rednose figured Coby had said too much, and now, they were down bad. Was he stupid enough to tell those RRG niggas that he had been the one that killed Carlos? Would Coby lie to make his enemies fear him? Rednose now had to figure out what all Cody said.

It would be stupid to give up your location, knowing that the whole city was looking for the killers of Carlos. Rednose knew Coby was his new shooter, but he wasn't that smart. That could hurt them.

"Coby, what did you tell the nigga?" Rednose questioned him with a serious demeanor.

"Told them fuck niggas we ain't ducking no smoke! He called me saying Cee Money said she saw me with you at the mall last week. I just told them niggas pull up. Ion do no argument shit!" Coby confessed.

"Nigga, is you stupid? You could of got your sister killed. You didn't learn nothing from the last incident? Use your brain, homie. This shit is chess, not checkers." Rednose was getting upset the more he spoke, so he got quiet.

Then, Coby continued. "To keep it real, I made a YouTube video, dissing RRG and Carlos, big bra. I knew you was going to be mad, but I didn't show my face. I had on a Pooh Shiesty ski mask and all-black gloves on. I shot the video where the body was found hanging," Coby confessed, now realizing how stupid he was.

"Who shot the video?" Rednose asked. He kept his disappointment hidden for the moment because he needed real answers to restore safety. If he started yelling and screaming at Coby, he would not get the response he wanted, so he just remained as calm as possible. The fact that Ebony almost got shot because of her brother really had Rednose looking at Coby differently.

"My partner, Trey Vando, did the video. Why?" Coby asked. Rednose was about to tell him that his partner was dumber than him for recording it and uploading it to his YouTube channel. He was also going to advise Coby that his partner was probably dead or about to die soon.

All of a sudden, something hit Rednose. The cars didn't park and walk down on them, meaning they didn't park the car and get out on foot like most drills were done in the city these days. So, that meant they were about to spin the block again. This time would be with fully automated weapons, and somebody was going to get hit up.

"Back door now! Ebony, come on. Let's go, Coby! Them fuck niggas about to spin back around," Rednose demanded as he led the way toward the back door. They were opening the back door when the shots came in. It was louder and sounded like more weapons than last time.

Blatttttttttttttttttttttttt!

To Rednose, it sounded like fully automatic gunshots ripping up the sheetrock.

As they made it out the back, Rednose noticed Ebony was walking funny before she stumbled and fell. She had been shot somewhere in her back. That was when Rednose lost his mind. He rushed around the side of the house and took aim at the last car. He shot several shots at the tires. The other two cars were speeding away, but the last car had sparks coming from the back right tire area. First, the car began to swerve from side to side. Next, it crashed into a mailbox.

"Yeah, fuck niggas, let's play *Call of Duty!*" Rednose yelled as he started running toward the car.

Coby was holding Ebony in his arms while calling the police to get his sister some help. He thought about giving chase along with Rednose, but he couldn't just let his sister bleed out by herself like that.

Rednose shot at the car, hitting the back window. Next, he saw two niggas jump out the car and take off, running around. He ran behind them, sending shots. One of them ducked down and jumped behind a parked truck. He pulled out his gun and shot back.

This forced Rednose to get low as well then run into a yard. He got behind the closest object to take cover. It was a big power generator. The nigga behind the truck popped out and began to shoot in his direction. It was evening time, so it wasn't even dark yet. These two niggas shot at each other for over ten minutes. It was like one of those YouTube videos where both of them were trying to shoot for their life at one point. With more aggression and vengeance pumping through him, Rednose began closing in on him, whereas the other guy was trying to get up out of there.

Finally, Rednose shot him in his lower body somewhere because he dropped instantly and grabbed his leg. Rednose ran directly over to him and shot him twice in the face, no talking or hesitation. Next, he ran back as fast as he could to get back to Ebony and Coby. As he ran, he heard somebody come outside and scream. He knew the police would be there at any second. He finally made it back to the spot.

Rednose's heart dropped. Ebony wasn't moving, and Coby was just standing there, crying. Rednose's anger overtook him. His adrenaline was already rushing, and Coby just standing by Ebony's body, just looking scared, was the dumbest thing he could do. He didn't apply any pressure to her back with a towel or anything. So, she'd just been sitting there, losing blood. Rednose ran straight inside and grabbed the nearest cloth. It was a big towel. He sat Ebony up and saw she was hit once in the back. He slowly wrapped the towel around her.

"Here, take my keys and go bring the whip around back and hurry up. We going to take her to the hospital," Rednose yelled.

"I called the ambulance. Th-they on th-the way," Coby said stupidity and nervously. He was talking crazy.

"Fuck no. We not waiting, stupid ass boy. If she die, I'ma kill yo lil fuck ass. Got her out here just bleeding until she passed out. Now you talking about waiting on the ambulance. She will not make it, nigga!" Rednose pointed the Glock at Coby as he ranted.

"My bad. I didn't know," Coby cried out as he ran to get the car.

When Coby pulled up, Rednose slowly carried Ebony to the car. He laid her in the backseat and got in behind her, and Coby sped off. Rednose didn't see anybody in the car he'd made crash. So, he knew they all got away except the one he'd walked down on. He looked at Ebony, and he noticed her body was cold.

Chapter 11

Ebony stayed in a coma for less than a week then she opened her eyes. Rednose was right there waiting on her. Afterwards, it took her another few weeks to practice walking around again. First, she had to walk with a walker because she didn't have any strength in her back. They were able to remove the bullet out of her back, but it still did some damage. The doctors were skeptical at first. As Ebony came out of the coma and began to walk upright again, they knew she would make a full recovery.

"What is that smell? I was just dreaming about some hot food!" Ebony said as Rednose returned to her room with a bag of hot food.

He sat the food down then went over to adjust the bed. When he pulled out the plates of food, Ebony's whole facial expression brightened up. Steam came from her food as she opened the plate.

"Oh, my goodness. I haven't had any homemade food in weeks. Wow, where did you get this from?" Ebony stared at the food, smiling.

There was cheesy macaroni, barbequed chicken, deviled eggs, muffins, yellow, spicy cheese rice, and collard greens with neck bones. He also had a big cup of sweet iced tea.

"My mama cooked yesterday. I just heated your food up and put you a big plate together. You need to get your strength back and get your weight back up," Rednose spoke as he watched Ebony eat her food. It was so good that she didn't even respond to him. Normally, she would when he said something about her loss of weight.

Rednose had finally gone to visit his mother and sister. They were happy to see him but mad because he didn't tell them he was out. His sister immediately pulled up to their mom's house when she was called and notified that her brother was sitting at the dinner table. She came straight inside and smacked him across the head.

Then, she cried and ran into his arms.

They ate, and all three of them had a very long conversation. It was the most they had talked since before Rednose went to prison. They discussed the situation with Marcella, Rednose's older brother who he refused to speak on. They discussed money that was stolen from him. They discussed him leaving them by themselves by going to prison. They discussed why he was never going to reach out to his brother. It was a lot of personal things that needed to be discussed. The love was still very much there. Sometimes, it just took time for family matters to work out. However, Rednose did advise his family that he was in danger, and he wouldn't be able to be around them for the time being. He was smart enough not to put the most important people in his life in harm's way. When karma came back around, he didn't want his family anywhere near.

He looked up and saw Ebony enjoying her food. His mind began to wonder. What if she would have gotten killed? He had been moving real reckless since he came home. Anger had outweighed his wisdom. There was no reason he should have done all the wild and unforgettable things he did. With so much anger and hatred built up, with revenge and heartbreak driving you mad, you did things that would make you regret them later in life. Seeing the pain he caused Ebony made him regret everything.

Ebony and Rednose had just slept in the same bed the night before she was shot. Rednose had been the only man she'd been with since her first. It all started off with them drinking and talking all night. See, Ebony and Rednose had always been friends with each other. He never saw her outside of the friend zone, but the more time they spent together, the closer they became.

She saw Rednose as a big brother type influence. Never did she think they would end up having sex. Rednose saw it as more than sex. The liquor made him realize how sexy Ebony was. Her body was fine, and her ass was juicy like a peach. She didn't post all the half-naked pictures on the internet. She wasn't caught up in all the street drama, and she carried herself like a real lady. This proved to Rednose that she wasn't a thirsty bitch seeking attention and validation. She was the type that you kept on your side. She even went out of her element to hold Coby and Rednose down, and that nearly cost her her life. That made him want to protect her even more. He felt like he let her down. He got her involved, and she'd warmed him about everything ahead of time, even tried to warn him about Cee Money and the trouble she could cause. Now, he felt like he owed her everything.

Rednose still wasn't talking to Coby. Every time he walked in Ebony's hospital room, Rednose would leave. He didn't want to even look at him. How could he be so naïve? He had Ebony just lying there, bleeding. If Rednose would have gotten shot by the opps or worse, Ebony could have died. Doctors said she almost lost enough blood to cause severe brain damage. So, when Rednose was finally sure Ebony was recovering fully, he would have to groom Coby better. They could not afford to get caught slipping like that again. That was the easiest way to lose a war. Why would you tell your enemies where you were staying?

Coby was still hurt over the death of his girlfriend. Now that Ice Water was back out, he wanted to make him feel his pain. That was why he claimed responsibility for Carlos' death. He didn't use all his brain cells. If he did, he would have known that he was only putting his sister in the same danger he had put his girlfriend in.

You couldn't be in the streets, beefing with people and giving out locations. Also, you had to protect your family and especially the females at all costs. What you did in the streets would come to your house. The people you loved the most would get hurt. You had to really know what you were getting yourself into before you jumped into a situation thinking you were tough.

One day, Rednose stood outside Ebony's hospital room and heard Coby break down and start crying very hard. Ebony was sleeping due to the meds. Coby started saying how sorry he was and that he wasn't thinking. He promised to stop using drugs and change his life if she made it. He told her he still dreamt about his girlfriend that Ice Water shot to death, and he was going to make those niggas pay for hurting the two women he loved the most. After he did that, he promised to make a change. Rednose walked off but kept it in his mind to groom the young man and really give him some wisdom. He could tell that Coby had a good heart, but he was still young and dumb. The boy had heart and a lot of nuts, but bravo only made you an easy target in the art of war. He was going to get his mind right. If he didn't, they did not have a chance of surviving in the city. Word was out now, and it was only a matter of time before it went up.

"That was so good, Rednose. I can eat that every day," Ebony spoke out loud. Her voice made Rednose snap back to reality. He had zoned out like he did when in deep thought.

"When you moving out of town?" Rednose asked as he slightly grabbed her hands.

"I really don't know," Ebony said, unsure of her comment. She didn't have any money, and her job was in the city. Rednose read her mind. He already knew she would be skeptical.

"Don't worry about any money. I got you. Your job is not safe anymore. We are not safe in this city anymore," Rednose confessed. He continued to tell her the plan he had come up with since she'd been in the hospital. It seemed like he was making new plans every few months, and none of them seemed to be going well for him. It was like the more he tried to get away, the deeper he was pulled in.

"What about my brother?" Ebony asked. Her heart was big.

"His lil bitch ass coming with us. I should of never got y'all involved with this shit. I'ma fix it. I promise you that. Until then, I need you safe, so we going to be living right outside the city for a few months. Me and Coby will slide to the city to handle business, but you are out of this," Rednose stated as he rubbed her shoulders gently.

"I'm not going to disagree with you, but I actually want to put some of my target practice to use. Them bastards shot up our place and shot me in the back. I'm still weak, and I had to rebuild my lower body strength. Good thing I used to play volleyball and exercise because this shit painful as fuck. However, I will let you guys do what you do best. I don't want y'all going out there against all odds, but I understand there is nothing I can say or do that will stop you and Coby from seeking justice. I just wished you would of listened to me when you first got from prison."

Ebony stopped talking because tears started falling. Rednose just held her head on his stomach as he stood over her. They remained in silence for a while, both deep in their thoughts.

This was all a serious reality check for Rednose. What would his future be like? Would he end up in the streets, shooting and robbing? Would he move to the West Coast and start his production company? Would he go back to jail? Would he get caught for the murders he'd committed since he'd been out of prison? Would the streets get him before he got them?

He knew he was in too deep in a danger situation, so he was going to have to make some life changes or continue to roll the dice with his life. He couldn't just walk away right now. It wasn't because he had something to prove. He did not care about what anybody thought of him. All that went away when he was left for dead in prison. He knew people were fake and just played cool if it was beneficial. He couldn't walk away because he needed to get his get back. It was just in his competitive nature. He refused to accept defeat, even if he was down three to one like LeBron in 2016. He was going all in. He was back in that mode.

Chapter 12

The new house was set up with security cameras all around it. It was also located within a very upscale, gated community. Furthermore, there was an extra fence built around the house. There would be no drive by shootings going on in this neighborhood. Neighborhood Watch was on security twenty-four hours a day. That included three different eight hour shifts. The small town was less than fifty miles outside of Columbus, Georgia.

It took Ebony another few months to regain all of her strength, but she was back to moving around good now. It took another few months to convince Rednose she could work. So, she finally got a job working twelve hours a day, making twenty dollars an hour. Coby also had a job working in a warehouse. Rednose didn't need to work. He still had plenty of money that he never told anyone how he was able to develop. Ebony believed that he was flipping his money he'd saved up while in prison. She always saw him reading things about investing and trade markets. He had become a wizard online. He owned several laptops and was on them daily like a desk job.

Coby and Rednose were always taking trips to the city to scope out the scene to see how things were going. Coby had people he would contact to get the word on the streets. Lately, there had been way too much drama to keep up with, so much drama that Carlos' case wasn't even that mind blowing anymore.

Rednose never let him get information from only one person. He would make him check with at least two of his other sources before he even considered the rumors. One of the rumors was that Coby was the leader of the RRG Killers gang. He was the one that hung Carlos, and the video he'd made dissing them had gotten almost one million views in less than a year. The reason he did this to Carlos was because Ice Water had shot him and killed his girlfriend. According to the street's rumors, Ice Water and some of the RRG members had spun the block on Coby and killed his sister and ran him out the city.

A RRG member who called himself Bandlab (because he kept a drum) had gotten killed after Coby and his crew had returned fire and flipped one of the getaway cars. This led up to RRG members going after Trey Vando, the local film director, because he shot the video of Coby disrespecting Carlos. Trey Vando was guilty by association. One day, he was shooting a video for another group who called themselves Gravediggers. Ice Water and a group of RRG members slid through and shot that shit up viciously. Three people were killed, including Trey Vando. The strange twist was that Mook was a popular member of the Gravediggers. That was how Rednose found out that Mook was back out and getting active. Mook and his Gravediggers gang were in daily shootouts with Ice Water and the RRG members. This would end badly for Mook. He would have been better off hanging with his flunkies in the county jail.

The city had multiple wars going on, and the police were lost and didn't know who shot who. It was somebody getting shot almost every day. The sad part was that those motherfuckers didn't have any honor amongst thieves, meaning females and children were caught in some of the crossfire. Ice Water was even bragging about how he shot someone's mother by accident.

No murder case had been solved in over fifteen months. The most brutal case was a triple homicide involving three females that were shot leaving the mall. Inside the mall, two gangs were shooting at each other. So, the people in the mall ran around in panic. A few people were shot in the mall, but it got deadly during the escape. Three young females were driving away, trying to get around cars. One of the gang members pulled out a Draco and shot at his opps that were driving next to the three young ladies.

With no remorse, he sent bullets through several cars and shot wildly with no aim due to the kick back from the baby AK. When the smoke was clear and everyone was gone, the only car that wasn't moving was the car with the three young ladies. One was in high school, one was in the military, and the other one was pregnant. All three were hit at least twice. The gang members that he was aiming for didn't get shot once. Tragic.

The city was torn to pieces. Everybody was heartbroken. The shouts and protests of, "Stop the violence," were trending. The mayor and police chief were under fire. The GBI and Feds were taking over and arresting all the popular troublemakers. They were trying to get the guns off the streets. They were pushing the narrative of gun control.

Most of the beef was petty and overrated. You had people losing their lives over literally nothing. It was the revenge factor that enhanced the ongoing gun battles. So many females were money hungry that they would switch up on the man they loved in twenty-four seconds. These city girls were more dangerous than the actual gang bangers. You couldn't trust any of them, no matter how cute they were. That was how Mook ended up eliminating himself off of Rednose' hit list.

According to the street rumors, Mook was found dead in a hotel room across from the strip club off of Victory Drive. At first, the female he was with was missing. Then, word came out that she skipped town when the Gravediggers found out she set Mook up. The streets were saying Ice Water paid her $2,500 to seduce Mook and spike his drink then invite him to her hotel room. It worked. Unfortunately for Mook, a staged robbery turned into a murder. He thought it was a robbery until Ice Water took off his mask and smiled at him before putting a bullet hole between his eyes.

Mook was found dead the next day with his pants still down. Those dog ass city girls would set up their own baby daddy. You could walk in the club and see the money hungry vibes from the female vultures. Mook had eliminated himself. That was when Rednose realized the name of the game was survival.

Whoever could last the longest won. It would be a wise choice, not a coward decision. He decided to sit back and let his foes eliminate themselves. He laid low for months and months, just stacking money and flipping it on his online betting and investing. He would still slide through the city without warning to go visit his family and to go scoop up Coby's new girlfriend, Alexis. He loved to spend time with his nephews and baby sister. He also couldn't get enough of his mother's hot plates. Him and his family were getting closer even though he stayed miles away.

One day, he had a cookout for the crew. It was only him and Ebony, Coby and Alexis, his mother, baby sister, and nephews. He had the grill going in his backyard. His mother was impressed with the big property and nice house. The smoke on the grill made it smell and feel like home. It was one of the best days he'd had since he'd been home.

Another good time was when he took Ebony and Coby to a football game in Atlanta. The next day, they went to see LeBron James play the Atlanta Hawks. Coby was so happy because Rednose let him wear some of his jewelry. They spent that weekend having a good time in Atlanta. They went to a club to party. Ebony was dressed in a nice pink bodysuit with matching pumps. Her body was so nice. She was beautiful, and Rednose had helped her regain her confidence after the nasty scar on her back began to fade away.

Everything had been going well lately; however, that didn't last too long. Rednose went to visit his mother and found out that a detective had come by to ask to speak to him. He wasn't shocked but definitely worried. He began to wonder if he'd left any crime scene messy. He was very nervous about the Carlos situation. He still had nightmares about that whole ordeal.

Nobody knew, but around that time, Rednose was dealing with a drug addiction. So, he was wigging out on the things he did to Carlos. He knew he'd gone too far, but it was a demonic thing that had possessed him. He also wanted to become the nightmare to all the niggas in the city who had forgotten about him. He wanted revenge for Cee Money. He was acting out of anger and rage. Now that he was drug free, he didn't feel the same way. He was ready to end his hit list and start looking for a place in California, probably the Bay Area. San Francisco was right up his alley. First, he had to take out RRG's main shooter, and that was Ice Water.

He was going around bragging about how he was the one who killed Coby's girlfriend and his sister, Ebony. He also said he ran the RRG Killers out of the city. This young nigga said he killed Mook, and those Gravediggers niggas saw him in the club every weekend and didn't want no smoke. He was bragging about all this live on his Facebook. The city had a lot of dislike and fear for him. A bunch of young idiots praised him. Watching Ice Water's live videos and hearing his music made Rednose realize a lot about himself.

He no longer wanted to be top dawg in the city. The streets were different; the rules were not followed. Snitching was okay now. Killing children and females was accepted. Violence and money made people worship you. Negative energy was winning.

Rednose wanted to find a way to go against that whole trend. To do so, he had to leave the small town he grew up in. He used to love the city and could go anywhere. Now, he barely visited his hometown. Almost everybody he knew was dead or in prison or doing junkie stuff. He wasn't going to have a bad ending even though he committed bad acts. He was going to make his good outweigh his bad. That was one reason he had been lowkey donating money to foster care foundations and making sponsorship payments to homeless shelters. The sad part about it was that wasn't going to stop the circle of death. What he didn't know was that Cee Money was behind the scenes cooking up a money hungry plot to get back at him for leaving her for Ebony and killing the man she truly loved, Carlos.

Chapter 13

Ebony was in the kitchen making the guys breakfast plates, while Rednose and Coby were downstairs playing *NBA 2K*. She loaded both of their plates because she knew how they ate, especially after smoking the early morning wake and bake. There were fluffy biscuits, fried sausage, cheese grits, boiled eggs, waffles, steak patties, and cups of orange juice. She had to go to work in a few hours, so she had cooked early. They would have to order Door Dash for dinner because she wasn't going to be home.

Rednose was downstairs, beating the shit out of Coby. He had won four straight games by at least ten points. They also had $200 on each game, so Coby was down $800. Rednose was determined to get him out of a whole grand because he disrespected the goat, LeBron James.

"That nigga old. He like fifty years old, brah. Ain't no way he still dunking the ball that hard. This nigga on steroids or something," Coby complained.

"Shut the fuck up, pussy! And one!" Rednose yelled as he scored an easy bucket with LeBron and got a foul call as well.

Rednose ended up beating him again, this time by twenty points. Coby gave Rednose his money and finally gave up. They went upstairs to eat breakfast. They both hugged and kissed Ebony, telling her like always how good the food was. After they all finished eating, Ebony got in the shower and ready for work. Coby was on the phone with his new girlfriend. Rednose had business to handle.

First, he had to order his film equipment and meet with this white guy named Ryan who would possibly be his new cameraman and director. Rednose was ready to start filming his show series. His idea for his first season did not require a large cast.

He would not need anything besides a few public settings. His first show was about a terrorist attack from the Russians that was targeted to the city water companies. This poison in the water caused seventy percent of the country to get wiped out. The other thirty percent were immune to the affects. When the first episode began, it would be shot seven months after the first attack. Rednose was alone in a small town, trying to survive.

This was only one of his ideas that made him want to go to the biggest stage in California.

He wanted to have his own camera crew and cast members. He was going to try to come up independent. He was also willing to work with industry veterans. He had his own money to invest in the low budget shows. He remembered reading that the movie, *Quiet Place*, was very cheap to film and had become a thriller. Rednose was almost ready to start hiring cast members that were willing to act out scripts he had written and already had the concept down pat.

Later on that morning, Rednose heard Coby on the phone, yelling something about having the drop on Ice Water. When Rednose walked in on him, Coby began to explain that his people had called him and announced they had discovered that Ice Water's mother was a cook at Golden Corral. Rednose couldn't believe this shit. Ice Water was running around disrespecting dead people, killing women, and flexing all his money on the internet, yet his mother was a cook in a public restaurant. Any of his enemies could snatch his mother up with ease. Rednose didn't believe it was that simple. Or if it was true, that meant that this new generation wasn't really trying to get at him for real. Rednose knew the city was afraid of the image that Ice Water had. The young nigga wasn't taking his enemies seriously because his mother was very touchable.

RRG was supposed to be a money clique, but ever since Ice Water came home from prison, it had been nothing but gun slanging. He claimed it was revenge for Carlos. That didn't explain all the other beefs and shootouts that he had gotten RRG in as of late.

As another twist to this already messy situation, Cee Money was pregnant. The word on the street was that Ice Water was fucking her too. Yes, she was a certified dog. Those city girls were so money hungry that they would switch up on you in less than twenty-four seconds. All you had to do was have some money and shoot your shot. Finding out Cee Money was pregnant didn't surprise Rednose. This also confirmed that she was indeed trying to trick him with the picture of the fake pregnancy test. Ebony was right. Cee Money had a death wish. Although Rednose did want to kill her for setting him up, he decided to let the streets eat her. He did a special prayer and knew her karma was going to wrap her in a circle of death real soon.

"We can slide to the city this weekend and snatch that nigga moms up and make him give himself up for her," Coby said, and he looked so focused and dangerous. Rednose hadn't seen this side of him that often.

Coby really wanted Ice Water dead, and Rednose knew why. He took the girl he loved away from him. Jealousy made him kill her. He was mad because she chose Coby instead of him. Coby really wanted to get revenge. He even kept pictures of her all on his dresser. Rednose wanted to end this once and for all. He already wasn't even on that beef with RRG anymore, especially once he realized how he got tricked into a battle over a no-good ass, gutter rat, disloyal bitch. The last straw was getting rid of Ice Water. After that,

Coby would be able to go visit his girlfriend's grave and say he sent her killer to hell. Rednose would be able to turn his life around and begin his career producing his films.

"We will snatch her up and make him pop out. This is how we going to do this." Rednose proceeded to lay out the plan.

Chapter 14

Ebony was just getting home from work when a police car followed her in the neighborhood. She didn't think much of it until it followed her all the way to the driveway. When she got out of the car, the window of the police car came down, and the officer asked to speak to her. Rednose was peeping out the window. The officer and Ebony spoke for less than ten minutes before he drove away. Ebony had anger in her eyes as she entered the house. Rednose didn't say anything until she called his name and asked to speak to him about something.

"Okay, this is too much," she said while shaking her head in regret.

"What's too much, baby? What are you referring to?" Rednose asked with a calm demeanor.

"My mother sent the police here to see if I was being forced to stay here in this town against my will." Ebony started crying.

Ever since Ebony was shot, she hadn't been back to Columbus at all, and her family was worried. She and Rednose talked for about an hour about this. This was when he found out that Coby was not her real brother. They didn't have the same parents. Coby didn't know his father, and his mother had overdosed when he was in YDC for stealing cars. Ebony's mother was actually Coby's godmother.

Ebony grew up a spoiled brat. She always had it easy and simple. She never had to really ask a man for any money, and her mother was very overprotective. So, since Ebony had been living out of town, her mother was afraid she was being controlled by a man. Ebony only FaceTimed her mother. They shared locations, so that was how she was able to get the address and send the cops to the new house. Rednose paid, but Ebony's name was on everything.

So, it was her house as far as her mother was concerned.

This conversation revealed a lot of details about who Ebony was. Although when questioned by the detective in the hospital, she didn't cooperate, Rednose knew she wasn't really cut out for this type of lifestyle, and the tears running down her face confirmed it. Rednose knew she would fold if it came down to it, so he knew he had to make a change real soon. He told her they should take a break, and maybe she should go stay with her mother for a while. Having the police show up out of the blue was not cool at all to Rednose. He was selling illegal merchandise on the dark web and had military style weapons lying all around the house. If the cops would have asked to come in, it could have gotten ugly. He took this as a sign and knew he had to do something quick.

Rednose called Ryan and told him he was coming out to California where Ryan was at because he had a role in a local TV series being shot. Ryan had tried to get Rednose to join him, but Rednose didn't want to leave Ebony behind. Now, he was lowkey very upset and needed to get away asap before he said something that would hurt the poor girl's feelings.

"Bitch mama got the motherfucking police pulling up to my shit, talking bout she being held hostage in this big ass house... Man, I'm outta here!" Rednose said. He was outside on the porch later that day. He didn't realize that Ebony had overheard him.

Meanwhile, Coby was still plotting on snatching up Ice Water's mother. He had people in the city giving him updates. Ice Water's mother was an easy target, or so it seemed. Rednose kept telling Coby to just chill and wait.

Rednose wanted to lay low and wait for the right opportunity. Coby felt like Rednose was going soft on him. He was tired of waiting and was getting more anxious.

So, when Rednose told him that he was going to California for a few weeks and was leaving him the Trackhawk, Coby knew he was going to take a trip to the city. Rednose told Coby to be careful and not to fuck up his car. He should have told Coby not to go do anything stupid because that was exactly what he was going to do.

Three days later, Rednose landed in San Diego. It wasn't Los Angeles or San Francisco, but it was the closest he'd been. The air felt different, and he knew from the moment he got there that this was the right place to be. His energy was different, and he felt good. Ryan met him at the airport and chauffeured him around like he was on vacation or something. Rednose said fuck it and decided to spend some money. He went shopping and almost went broke on designer fashion. He couldn't help himself. All he had been doing since he got out of prison was negative and criminal activities. So, the first week in San Diego, he had a blast. Hanging with Ryan was different. Ryan had white friends he already knew, but when the Hispanic and Puerto Rican women showed up to a set, it surprised him. They went to an after party where the cast was shooting their first episode. Rednose enjoyed the VIP section. It made him feel like a movie star. This was the environment he belonged in. Maybe breaking away from Ebony was a blessing in disguise.

"Hey, Ryan, where is the restroom?" Rednose yelled over the pop music.

"Woah, too much champagne! Go downstairs and make a left. Walk down the hallway and follow the signs. You can't miss it," Ryan replied. He was super hyped. Maybe it was because of the blue eyed, blonde haired diva he had his arms around had him feeling dominant.

Ryan used to tell Rednose he was the man in California, but Rednose thought he was just capping and exaggerating.

Now, he saw those actresses loved them some Ryan. Rednose got up and walked carefully down the steps in his new Prada outfit. The place was packed with a mixture of Blacks, whites, and Hispanics. The DJ played a song by Bad Bunny, and the club went crazy. Even Rednose had to sway to the music. After he took a long piss, he checked his phone. He had seven missed calls from Ebony. He started to ignore the urge to return her call, but something told him to tap in just in case.

When Rednose got outside on the deck where he could hear better, he called Ebony back. By the trembling in her voice when she answered, he knew she had been crying. Ebony went on to tell him that Coby had gotten arrested after being caught on foot. He had gone to the city by himself, like Rednose always told him not to do, and gotten jammed up. He didn't get pulled over in Rednose's car; he was involved in a shootout inside of Golden Corral in Columbus, Georgia. The other suspects were also chased when two police cars arrived to the scene minutes after the shooting began. Ebony was saying that it was all over Facebook that Coby had tried to come shoot Ice Water's mother at her job, but Ice Water happened to be eating out there at the time, so when they saw each other, they both began shooting inside the restaurant.

That was the dumb shit Rednose was talking about. First, Ebony's mother called the police to come to the house out of town. Ebony just had to be sharing locations with her mother. Next, Coby took Rednose's car joy riding and went to do some crash dummy shit that he warned him to just lay low on. Now, Rednose had to help bond him out and find his car.

Rednose knew he could no longer continue on with Ebony and Coby. It was time for a new environment. That was when he bumped into someone trying to go past him.

He almost turned around to check the person for being close up on him like that when, all of a sudden, he saw it was a female. She had on all-white and was beautiful with long, black hair going down her caramel colored back. She was kind of skinny, but her body was very curvy. Her skirt was body hugging and cut up in a pop culture style. Rednose immediately got off the phone after telling Ebony he would have to call her back when he got back to Ryan's suite.

"Excuse me. I'm sorry, Beautiful," Rednose said to her, now taking in her breathtaking beauty. She had the baby face but the grown woman body.

"No, excuse me. I'm sorry. I just gotta get me some air before I lose my mind!" she replied back to him.

What began as a few minute's conversation turned into a long discussion. Rednose learned that some guy had ghosted her, and she was very mad about it. Rednose offered to hang out inside with her to get her mind off of it, and she accepted the offer. He led her back to the VIP area with Ryan and the crew.

At the end of the night, Rednose had her number, and they had plans on doing a lunch date the next afternoon. This was going to be a good start for Rednose because he was about to tell Ryan he didn't want to leave any time soon. Ryan suggested Rednose talk to the company about getting onboard. Ryan had connections, and maybe it could work out for him. This was what Rednose really wanted to do. Forget about being the top dawg of the city. That was a silly idea of the past. He even felt ashamed of himself looking back at it now and seeing the plan with Cee Money go wrong, things falling apart with Ebony, Coby getting arrested and not knowing if he was caught with weapons that were dirty or not, and all the bloodshed Rednose had created in the city because of Mook, Carlos, and his former friend, Dominque. There was also his part in killing the shooter who was involved with Ebony getting shot and all the hustling and long nights in solitaire. He knew now was the time to go be productive in life. He had no other choice. In twenty-four seconds, you could get set up by any money hungry city girl. Money was the only thing the streets were loyal to. Rednose decided to move to San Diego.

Chapter 15

Coby was riding down the street inside the car with his mother. He had finally made bond. Rednose still wasn't answering any of his calls. Something wasn't right, he began to think. Coby was not happy with Rednose because he felt like he was supposed to have gotten him out of there immediately. Instead, he stayed in there for weeks and was questioned more than once by different detectives. Coby's mother had asked what happened and how he'd gotten locked up. He didn't give her any details.

Coby started thinking about how things had gone down. While Rednose was in San Diego, Coby was in Columbus, Georgia. He had decided to go snatch up Ice Water's mother by himself. He wanted to prove to Rednose he was about that life now. He thought he could surprise Rednose with the news, but this was a bad idea altogether. As soon as Coby got inside of the restaurant, he ran into Ice Water and a few other RRG members who just happened to be there eating.

Ice Water jumped up and immediately opened fire in Coby's direction. Coby was able to duck behind the bar area and shoot back as well. They sent over seven shots back-and-forth. Surprisingly, nobody got shot. That was when Coby tried to run back to the car. It was trapped between two other cars trying to get out of the parking lot. Somebody started shooting at Coby, so he took off running down the hill for his life. He wasn't sure if Ice Water or any of the RRG members gave chase to him. A few blocks later, he ran slap into the police and got arrested.

Now, Coby had a pending case hanging over his head. He was feeling stupid now for not listening to Rednose about waiting for the right time before trying to snatch up Ice Water's mother.

He now realized how dumb it was for him to jeopardize everything. Now, his mother had to take out bank loans just to get him out on bond. The weapon he got caught with placed him at the restaurant shootout. Some of the bullets inside of Golden Corral matched the gun he was arrested with. He was questioned for hours about all kinds of things going on in the city. He couldn't believe the city was so dangerous now.

Word was out that Ice Water was looking for him and was going to blow his head off for trying to show up at his mom's job like that. People in the city were so afraid of Ice Water, and nobody could believe that Coby had survived a shootout again with someone like him. Coby didn't care about getting street credit anymore. He was just ready to end this beef by taking care of Ice Water.

Coby's girlfriend was even mad at him for ghosting her just to go get arrested. She was tired of the superhero role that Coby was trying to live. She just wanted to spend some time with him, and he kept causing problems every time he came around. She knew he was going to get himself killed doing all the stupid things he did. Like the time he shot the video where Carlos' body was found hanging from the tree. She warned him that the GBI would get him for questioning because he was making himself a suspect in a high profile murder case. He didn't listen and got his sister shot up and involved with another unsolved murder. Now, he just showed up and got caught up in a shootout inside of a restaurant.

When Coby got to his girl's apartment, she flat out told him what was on her mind. After she finished venting, she broke up with him for her own safety. She didn't want to put her life in danger anymore. She was tired of all the threats she would receive from people for dating him.

He had ruined a good thing. He wasn't going to find anyone as good as she was to him. She sent him money every week, wasn't cheating, and was down for him. The real reason she was breaking up with him was because she found out how his other girlfriend was killed. To think he was still beefing and having shootouts with the same guy that had shot him and killed his last girlfriend was a scary thought. Also, his sister had gotten shot up too. Yes, she was done with Coby's ass, and he knew it. Coby begged and begged, but he knew she was serious. He got in his car and drove away. Coby didn't realize how much he loved her until he felt the tears dropping down his face. He didn't want to be alone. He felt so lonely now. Rednose was still in San Diego, and Ebony was out of town. He didn't know if all the violence was getting to him or what, but it struck home when she broke up with him, leaving him fighting his own emotions alone.

That was when Coby called one of his old partners and decided to go ride around the city. They did, and that was not a good idea. There was a party going on on the south side. The name of Coby's partner, who was driving, was Peewee. Peewee was one of those young niggas who loved to pull up at all the major events such as parties and gatherings.

Coby didn't know who was having the party, but when he saw Cee Money, he knew he was in the wrong place. He immediately got Peewee's attention to leave, but he had been spotted. A cold chill ran throughout his entire body. He suddenly felt surrounded by enemies. As he looked around, he noticed RRG members inside the party.

He knew Cee Money was responsible for setting up Rednose, but he didn't know she ran with RRG and was as dirty as she was. Money hungry was the type of shit she was on. The only reason she was on those niggas' dick was because of the money they were making.

Coby finally found Peewee and explained to him why they had to leave. They managed to leave before anything could pop off. Cee Money had still seen Coby, and he knew how she got down. Coby had just gotten out of jail, and now, he was right back where his opps wanted him — an easy, outnumbered target. He had to begin to move a whole lot smarter if he wanted to survive. The moves he had been making lately damn sure weren't the smartest things he'd done in his life. He was actually lucky he wasn't dead. Now, he was in the city he was supposed to have been laying low and away from. Now, he was all alone and in danger.

Rednose had so much fun in San Diego that he didn't want to return. The flight back was over faster than it took him to get there. He would rather have stayed a few more weeks, but he had to handle business back home. Also, he needed to check on Ebony and Coby. He saw all the missed calls, but that didn't speed up his process. He didn't want to be linked to any jail call. Also, he reported his car stolen and didn't think about driving it again. He told Coby to be very mindful about the things he did without warning anyone. He continued to give Coby warning after warning. So, when he got himself caught up, don't call on Rednose. That was how Rednose looked at it. From his point of view, Coby was stupid and probably lucky to be alive.

Rednose got home and saw that the house was empty. That was weird, but he didn't think much about it. Ebony was back home with her mother, and Coby was probably still in Columbus with his girlfriend or doing something dumb as usual. Rednose knew he had to be on point from now on. Too much heat could tie him to something. He didn't feel safe around Ebony or Coby anymore. He was about to start planning on moving to San Diego and start doing business with Ryan. They were going to start filming Rednose's TV series.

Ebony didn't answer the phone on the first call, so he sent her a text message. She finally called back about twenty-five minutes later. That was when she explained to Rednose that she was living with her ex-girlfriend now and was going to try to work things out with her. Rednose wasn't that angry, but he was surprised at the new energy. He didn't know Ebony could have a whole mood swing like that out of nowhere. Now, she was basically telling Rednose she was moving on to a new relationship and no longer wanted to wait for him to work things out.

Rednose had to accept her decision and go on with his life. He didn't expect things to last that long with her anyway. Yet he didn't expect things to end so soon. Maybe it was best she did her own thing. Rednose could tell that she didn't like living all alone outside of the city. He just hoped she would be safe back in town now. A lot of people thought she was dead since the shootout. Rednose thought about putting up a fight and driving back to the city to ensure his girl's safety. He almost did but then soon realize she was safer without him in her life.

Being with him came with all kinds of challenges. So, now that she was gone, Rednose didn't have any reason to look after Coby anymore. But something told him he needed to save the young boy from the city and all the bad things that went wrong with situations like the one Coby was in. Rednose knew that if Coby didn't play it safe, he would be dead in less than a month back in the city.

Chapter 16

Coby was still out on bond, sitting in his mother's car on the passenger's side, eating a double cheeseburger from McDonald's. He could never forget how Rednose didn't answer his calls from jail. That made him look at Rednose totally different. He used to see Rednose as one of the toughest men alive. Not anymore. So, now he would be making decisions on his own now. He didn't need a big brother or big homie.

It only took Coby a few weeks to assemble a small group of his childhood friends. They all believed his story about how he kidnapped and hung Carlos. Also, he was living off the hype of running up in Golden Corral and shooting it out with Ice Water and his crew. Coby's name was back blazing in the city. Even a few females started acting like groupies and began flirting with him all over the internet. Back in the day when he was in the rap game, his music was getting good views, and he had some flunkies still following him around. They were younger than all the other rival gang members.

"Coby, let's hit this party up on the south side," Jack Boi yelled over the music. They were riding through the city and looking for something to get into.

"What party?" Coby asked him. He hit a blunt as he listened to Jack Boi explain.

Coby had been out of town, so the new popular girls throwing parties were surprising to him. Jack Boi continued to explain how the parties had everyone pull up, and all the baddies were up in there.

So, Coby and his crew decided to slide through. Coby was a little skeptical because the last time he went out to a public event in Columbus, he saw some RRG members and had to get out of there fast. He wasn't going to let anyone keep him away from all the new young pussy.

Meanwhile, Rednose was at the house by himself, working on the dark web. He'd been packing up all his equipment and electronics. Next, he was going to pack up all his clothes and leave for good. The car Coby had left abandoned in Columbus, Rednose had reported it stolen as well. He had some more wheels and was about to get on the road soon. He did not have any plans besides relocating and laying low. Ebony and Coby were now out of the picture, and Rednose wanted to leave the state altogether.

Suddenly, his phone started ringing. It was Cee Money. He didn't answer. He didn't know what to think. How the fuck did she get his number? She called back, and he answered this time.

"I know you don't fuck with me like that anymore, but I still love you. Look, you probably don't trust nothing I say but trust me on this. The young boy going around the city saying you paid him to slide on Carlos because of me," Cee Money explained.

Rednose just started laughing. He knew that the young boy she was talking about was nobody but Coby. Now, he was going to be a problem. At that moment, Rednose realized he had to get rid of Coby. Also, he really believed that Coby had said something to the police to get out all fast and shit.

"How did you find out this information, and how do you know they talking about me?" Rednose asked, fishing for more details.

Cee Money was quiet at first, as if she was gathering her thoughts, before she continued to answer.

"The young boy name is Coby, and he said you was fuckin his sister, Ebony." Cee Money went on to reveal that she knew a lot of information. Coby had been running his mouth, and that was unacceptable.

When Rednose finally got off the phone with Cee Money, she had tried to get him to link up with her, but he declined. She must have been crazy to think she would get another opportunity to set him up. Bitch, please.

She was good for something. Rednose now knew that Coby wanted him dead and was going around the city bad mouthing him at parties for clout. He was a clout chaser and just wanted to make it look like he was dangerous and on demon time. Truth be told, he was a scared little boy and almost let his sister bleed out because he was so inexperienced. Rednose knew he could not let Coby know he was coming for him. Rednose also couldn't tell Ebony anything at all about his recent discovery.

Cee Money said there was a lot of money for the person who was able to track down and kill Carlos' killer. Rednose had to come up with a bounce back plan before he hit the city to go to war. He didn't expect Coby to trade on him. He didn't expect Coby to be loyal either. He didn't know what to expect; however, he did know how things were going to end — real bad for Coby.

Chapter 17

Rednose decided to pop out and hit the city. He had all of his property in storage out of town. The house was left nearly empty. Earlier, Ebony had reached out to him. After a long discussion, she revealed something to him. It was Coby. She said he was living very dangerously since he'd gotten out of jail. She also said somebody had shot her mother's house up, but fortunately, nobody was inside.

Ebony told him she had spoken to Coby's girlfriend. The girlfriend told Ebony that she wasn't with Coby anymore, but he wasn't trying to let her go. Coby had become very aggressive and was stalking her. Ebony asked Rednose to come pick her up because she wanted to see him.

Before he got on the road, Rednose got a phone call from a number he didn't recognize. At first, he wasn't going to answer, but the number kept calling. As soon as he answered, some niggas started talking crazy. He was saying things like, "Nigga, you out of prison now, out here running around ducking smoke. Show your face. You a dead body walking, zombie ass nigga." Rednose disconnected and blocked that number.

Rednose thought he recognized some of the voices that had just called his number to threaten him. He really couldn't pinpoint who they were because he had been involved with so much beef and violence with different niggas since he'd gotten out. He had been keeping a low profile for over a year, but he figured now was the perfect time to pop out.

Coby had put it out there that Rednose was out of prison even though he was going around claiming all of Rednose's murders. How dumb could you really be to make yourself the suspect in unsolved murder cases? Rednose knew the way he displayed things to Coby could one day backfire. He didn't know the young boy was so stupid. He wanted to be a tough guy so bad. Now, Rednose was going to see how tough he really was with some hot lead in his body.

It was going to break Ebony's heart, but Rednose was going to put Coby to sleep and close his mouth permanently. What Rednose didn't know was that Coby wasn't alone anymore. He had a group of young niggas that were dumber than him. They were all ready to crash out and lose it all just for a name in the streets. Rednose didn't care who was with Coby. When he pulled up, they better be ready.

Rednose decided to meet Ebony at Steak and Shake restaurant on the north side of town. They ordered their food without much talk. After they ate, they began to talk about how things had been lately. Ebony revealed that Coby had been moving real recklessly as of late. She was afraid that he was going to lose his life, and she wanted Rednose to help talk some sense in him. Rednose didn't say anything out loud but talking to Coby was the last thing he was going to do for the young boy. People were calling Rednose's phone now and threatening him all because Coby couldn't keep his mouth closed.

Ebony told Rednose that Coby and his friends hung out at the studio on the east side all the time. Rednose told her he would try his best to catch up with Coby but knew he was lying. Also, Ebony kept saying she missed him and hated how things ended. She didn't want to leave him, but she was tired of living like that. Rednose didn't blame her. He was tired of living like that himself. All he wanted to do was move to San Diego and start a new life.

"So, Rednose, what girls you been talking to?" Ebony asked him while folding her arms, waiting for his reaction.

"Why does it matter? You left me for a girl, right?" Rednose replied sarcastically.

"Don't do all that now," Ebony complained.

They continued to talk for a while before Rednose promised to get with her later on after he went to see his mother and sister. He kissed Ebony on her cheek before he got inside his car and sped away. Ebony sent him a text message saying not to forget about her as he continued to drive away. He stopped at a gas station to fill up. Once he was exiting the gas station, someone called his name. It was a female's voice. He looked to the left and notice a redbone with short hair calling out to him. Once he got closer, he still didn't recognize who she was.

"So, you don't remember me?" The female started laughing then pulled out her cell phone. She went to a picture. "Look at this photo from this old concert and see if you recognize me better," she said and passed him the phone.

When Rednose saw the picture, he instantly remembered it. It was way before he went to prison, back when he was very popular and the city was his. The girl standing next to him was someone he hadn't seen in a very long time. Her name was Kiki, and he had known her for a while. The reason he didn't recognize her was because she had lost so much weight.

"Kiki! What's good, baby girl? How you been?" Rednose yelled out loud and gave her a big hug. Kiki couldn't stop laughing and smiling. She was blushing like a schoolgirl.

"I know I look different. I lost all that baby fat, boy," Kiki responded.

The two of them decided to exchange numbers. Rednose told her to text him later on because he had to go see his family, but after that, he wasn't doing anything, so they could catch up. She agreed before she drove away.

As Rednose drove away, he thought about the last time he saw Kiki and what all took place.

It was on a Friday night on the east side of town. Rednose was the man in the city, and everybody was all on his wave. Kiki and some of her friends were the best looking group of ladies at the function. Rednose and his crew approached them, and Rednose ended up getting Kiki's phone number. He was supposed to call her, but he ended up getting arrested for a bunch of charges he had pending. So, he never got a chance to link up with Kiki. She seemed to remember him real well, still having pictures on her social media from ten years ago. Rednose told Kiki he'd just gotten out of prison and had been in prison for ten years. Kiki was surprised but excited to be able to get another chance to talk to someone she used to have a huge crush on. They had exchanged numbers and gone their separate ways.

Rednose drove to his sister's apartment, thinking about the time he'd gotten arrested. He was just leaving the function on the east where he had met Kiki and her crew. As soon as he left, he noticed the police car behind him, but he didn't have a choice but to continue driving. The officer hit the lights and had him pull over by the Waffle House. He was charged with aggravated assault and possession of illegal firearms.

He was denied bond and was sentenced to thirty years. He served ten.

Rednose didn't feel like it had been ten years, but it had. It seemed like the time had gone by so quickly. Everything had changed in the city. All the younger niggas used to want all the bad bitches. Now, all those young niggas wanted to do was kill, kill, and more drills. Rednose knew he had outgrown that type of lifestyle, but somehow, he was still dragged back into it. First, it was with Cee Money and the money hungry plans. Then, there was the revenge list. Then, the beef with RRG was next. Finally, there was the situation with Coby. Negative events kept happening. Rednose knew he had to move.

"San Diego, brah? Why San Diego though?" Rednose's sister asked him once he explained that he was moving soon and the reason behind it.

"Yeah, San Diego, baby girl. I'm about to change my environment and upgrade my taste for women. I'm done with the ghetto, ratchet type shit going on in my life. I just wanna be happy and live stress free. I don't wanna have to be doing investigation and all the detective work, you feel me? When I get back on the West Coast, I'll call Nya," Rednose admitted.

"Nya? Who is that, brother?" His sister was smiling and happy that her brother had met someone new that had him interested.

"Nobody, just my friend that lives in San Diego. We met at a nightclub last time I went, and we been texting and shit like that. We made plans to get together when I go back. She got a rich and spoiled vibe, and it's something strange about her, but I'm kinda interested," Rednose confirmed.

After they finished talking, they went to their mother's house to eat. Mama always cooked when her children came to see her. The food made Rednose feel like he was at home and drama free. He wished things were that simple like when he was younger, his older brother would have a football game, and the whole family would go support. Then, afterwards, Mama would come home and cook a big dinner. Rednose wished things were like they used to be, but times had changed, and everything was different. Even if Rednose wanted to go hang out around the city, he couldn't because he didn't have any friends he talked to anymore. The ten years he'd done had separated him from all his childhood friends, and there was no reconnecting. Sometimes, Rednose felt lonely and in the world all by himself. The only male he really trusted was his older brother, and they had not been on speaking terms the last few years. They only checked on each other through their sister. Both had too much pride to apologize to each other, so they were both acting stubborn.

Later that night, Rednose took his sister back home and drove around the city, just thinking. He found himself thinking about Cee Money and what she had done to him. He still couldn't believe she had set him up. Now, she was calling him, trying to inform him. Rednose decided to keep her close and not reveal his true hate for her in order to gain more information. He thought about Coby as well. Ebony was not involved in the streets, so she didn't know Coby was really trying to get Rednose murdered. There was nothing to talk about when he saw Coby. It was up.

Chapter 18

Later on that night, Ebony and Rednose were lying in bed together, watching a movie on Netflix. Ebony's phone began ringing, so she answered.

"Hey, what's going on?" Ebony listened to the caller then said, "Okay, I'm coming."

Rednose decided to check his accounts while Ebony walked out of the room. Rednose didn't hear or see it coming. He was actually more shocked than hurt.

"What's up? Fight back! I've been waiting for this day. I knew I was going to catch you down bad. I've been laying on your bitch ass," yelled Coby as he ambushed Rednose with a flurry of punches.

Okay, so let's unpack this. Coby had called Ebony to open the door once he rode past her girlfriend's house and noticed someone else was there. He didn't know it was Rednose until he walked inside. All the rage and hatred he had immediately came out. He was very emotional and upset. It was funny he felt that way now because a few months ago, he felt the total opposite way about Rednose.

"That's all you got, nigga! You hit like a bitch!" Rednose said in between punches. Because he was under the cover when he was ambushed, he was not in a position to fight back, so all he could do at the moment was take the punches and trash talk.

Ebony was trying to get Coby to get off Rednose. Rednose was much stronger than Coby. Yet he was under a blanket. Coby wasn't weak and was big for his age, so it took a little effort to get out the awkward position. Once Rednose got up, he threw Coby across the room.

"My mouth bleeding! Oh, I'm finna beat your lil bitch ass, boy. I don't know what the fuck your problem is, and I been trying to spare yo lil police ass because I know you don't know any better!" Rednose began stomping and kicking Coby all in his face. Coby tried to stop the kicks, but Rednose was becoming more vicious with each kick.

Ebony was screaming for him to stop. When she saw he wasn't paying her any attention, she ran into the kitchen and grabbed a big pot. Without even thinking about it, she ran back inside the room and began swinging it in Rednose's direction. She hit him a few times in the back of the head.

"Ouch! Bitch, you crazy! Why the fuck you swinging that big ass pot at me like you lost yo motherfuckin mind?" Rednose grabbed the back of his head and rubbed the big ass knot that popped up instantly. He was also sweating and kind of out of breath. It had been months since he'd been to the gym, and at that moment, he realized he was out of shape.

"Coby, you have to leave now!" Ebony yelled, helping him up. Ebony was talking under her breath and was clearly frustrated.

"I'ma see you again! Next time, we not doing no fighting!" Coby yelled as he rushed out.

"Next time? No fighting? Nigga, what's up? You talking about gun smoke? You not bout that life! You little young ass street punk! Matter of fact…"

Rednose went from mad to outrageously angry after Coby had just made a threat in his face.

He rushed behind Coby and went to his car and went under his seat to grab his gun. Next, he popped the trunk and got his emergency weapon. He walked over to Coby, who was trying to get in his car and leave. He passed him one of the guns and just stared at him.

"Oh, my goodness! No, Rednose! Please! What are y'all doing?" Ebony was crying as she watched Coby and Rednose stare each other down, each pointing a weapon at the other.

Ebony didn't want it to come to this or come out in this way; however, she knew what Coby was going to do before he did it.

"You right. I'm not about that life. Here, you get your gun back. I don't want no problems." Coby was smiling in a slick way, like he knew a secret. He got in his car and began to leave.

Rednose put his guns away and stared at Ebony with surprise. He rubbed his knot again. He was about to say something to her until Coby stopped and yelled out his window a few words that would change everything Rednose thought he knew about Ebony.

"Rednose, if I was you, I would not be in the city, nigga. Everybody wants yo head. You came down here into a death trap just to chase behind a piece of pussy. Ebony, did you show Rednose that trick you do when you on top? This hoe got you so blind you had no idea we been fucking since day one. Your duck ass went for the brother and sister bullshit. You would of been better off with that money hungry slut, Cee Money. Now who laughing, fuck nigga? Go put some ice on that knot, duck ass nigga." Coby sped away, blasting drill music.

Chapter 19

Rednose could not believe that Ebony and Coby were undercover lovers on and off over the years. The fake brother and sister role was only an act. It all made sense why she hit him with the pot now. After Coby drove away, Ebony broke down crying and tried to explain everything to Rednose. He was so upset that he had to leave immediately before he did something that he would regret. Even though they weren't together anymore, it was the fact that she had been betraying him the entire time. It was giving Cee Money vibes all over again. Rednose knew for sure that he couldn't trust anyone now. Times were so different these days. You could be married to a bitch. Y'all could have a house, a dog, and two cars and never had an argument. Yet there was some dark secret she carried with her since she was seventeen years old. There was a nigga she would have in her heart that you could never replace. The only reason Rednose was so upset was because he hated getting outsmarted. Coby and Ebony had one up on him, and he was going to get back at both of their asses for the act of disloyalty.

For now, he had to head to the gym, so he could work off the frustration and get his energy back right. Once inside the gym, Rednose put his headphones on and selected his playlist before stretching. Next, he did seven sets of fifty pushups to get tight. Then, he hit the pullup bar and did ten sets of fifteen reps. He then got on the bike and worked his calf muscles out. After going hard for about thirty minutes, he was tired and out of gas. He still had energy but didn't feel like doing hard workouts, so he decided to drive to the gym and put some shots up.

When he got to the gym, he was surprised to see it was packed with hoopers. He sat on the bleachers and watched what was going on.

After a few minutes, it became obvious that a three on three contest was going on. They were doing full court too. It was just the vibe he needed to release all the tension. He noticed someone across the gym watching him. After they locked eyes, the guy made a beeline in Rednose's direction.

"Aye, bro, you wanna run with me next? We can pick up a third teammate from the losing team," the guy asked him.

"Yeah. Hell yeah. Let's do it," Rednose replied.

They continued to conversate about sports until it was time for them to hit the court. They picked up the best player from the losing team. The rules were for street basketball. They were playing to ten. A three pointer was counted as two, and two pointers were counted as one. Rednose hadn't played a pickup game of basketball since he was in prison, so the first few times up and down the court, he was playing like trash. After he got his groove, he began to cook their asses. His team went on to win three times in a row before they lost a game. Afterwards, he learned that the guy's name, who'd asked him to play with him, was Tony.

Tony said he was from Columbus and already knew who Rednose was. He said his name was being said a lot in the local music. Rednose was confused, so Tony asked Rednose if he wanted to hear the music his name was mentioned in. They went to Tony's car, and he played a video. Rednose was surprised to see Coby dissing him in a video.

"Coby! This lil nigga got a diss song about me? What the fuck?" Rednose laughed.

"Oh, you might wanna hear it," Tony said.

So, Rednose listened to it without any emotion. Afterwards, he asked Tony how he heard about the song.

Tony said it was trending on social media. The song was saying that Rednose paid Coby to kill Carlos over a bitch. Coby was still dry snitching and clout chasing. It was funny to Rednose because he knew it was all lies, but he didn't realize how dangerous it was for the rumor to circle the block twice before the truth even existed.

Rednose needed more information, so as he drove away from the gym to go shower at his sister's apartment, he called the messiest and most ghetto, ratchet person he knew.

"Hello. Hey, are you busy? I got a few questions." Rednose got straight to the point. There was no need for small talk at this point. If it wasn't for this bitch, he wouldn't even be involved in any of this ratchet ass shit anyway.

"Hey, what's up, Rednose?" Cee Money replied as if she didn't have any idea why he was calling her, which was cap.

"Have you heard the lil diss song lil buddy got out about me supposed to paid him to kill Carlos?" Rednose asked. As soon as he asked her, she began spilling the beans.

Cee Money told Rednose Coby was in the streets claiming all kinds of bodies. He was actually responsible for some — him and his little crew. He had rounded up some crash dummies and had them fooled like he was a real killer. So, they were out there doing drills for him. Ice Water and other RRG members were having shootouts with Coby and his little crew. So, bodies were dropping on both sides. Now, Coby was smart enough not to get caught in any cross fire but was the first one to go rap about it. He was more involved with the rap beef than actual beef. He had Rednose's name ringing so bad that everyone who didn't even know Rednose was dissing him in the city. Cee Money had even gotten shot at a local club. After that, she was staying in the house and trying to change her life. She even confessed that she did try to set Rednose up but only because RRG members had kidnapped her sister. She knew Rednose would never forgive her. She also admitted that Carlos was her man. They had been on and off for a while.

Now, she just wanted peace and to protect her family because things had gone too far. Rednose played her real close, but he was going to push her wig back.

"Bitch, you think you can admit to trying to get me killed, and I just let you live? Y'all hoes stupid as fuck!" Rednose yelled out loud after he got off the phone with her, getting angry just thinking about it. He was going to catch two more bodies then he was done with this city and the street life. Cee Money and Coby had to go. He couldn't even sleep at night thinking about it. He was ready to end this shit once and for all.

The next morning, he ate breakfast at his sister's apartment, then he told her he would be leaving town for a while soon. He left her a bunch of money and told her to make sure she sent their bother a nice amount. Then, he left.

Rednose noticed he'd left a few important things like cards with cash on them at Ebony's girlfriend's house. He was so mad about the situation with Coby and how she attacked him with the pot. He called her back-to-back, but she didn't answer, so he just decided to pull up, get his stuff, and leave.

When he got there, something didn't feel right. Ebony's car was in the driveway. He called her again, but there was still no answer. He knocked on the door. No answer. He could hear the commercials playing from a device inside, so he knew she was there.

"I don't have time for the bullshit. This hoe in her feelings. Bitch, I got shit to do!" Rednose yelled out before he decided to try to open the door. To his surprise, it was unlocked.

"Ebony, where my Gucci bag with my clothes I left?" he yelled out. Nobody responded, so he walked in her room.

"Oh, shit! What the fuck?!" Ebony was in a puddle of blood, eyes wide open in fear, dead on her bed.

Chapter 20

Lying in a puddle of her on blood, eyes wide open in fear, there was a bullet hole right between Ebony's eyes. Rednose's normal reaction was not to panic but gather his thoughts. The first thing that came to his mind was who'd done it, and the first person he thought of was Coby. But why? It didn't make any sense at all.

The next thing he thought of was to get his personal items out of the house and leave immediately. This was going to be more difficult than he expected.

The next thing that came over him was anger and sadness. As he began to look for his bag with his items inside, he didn't expect to feel tears burning his vision. Yes, Ebony had betrayed him and kept things from him, but she also saved his life before and had held him down for over a year. Things changed fast because he was just very upset with her for attacking him when he was fighting with Coby. Now, he wanted to find out what had happened to her and make it right.

There was a loud explosion.

"What the fuck?!"

All of a sudden, Rednose heard something explode, like a small grenade or something, which shocked the hell out of him. All the power in the house immediately went out. Luckily, it was still daylight outside. The explosion knocked him into the bedroom wall, causing a big knot to begin swelling in the back of his head. If he wasn't a hard head, he could have been knocked unconscious.

"Agggggh, fuck! I gotta get outta here!" Rednose said, looking at Ebony's dead corpse.

He noticed the house was ablaze now, but there was five times more smoke than fire. So, if he hurried, he had time to find his bag and leave. As you know, Rednose was very big on his intuition. Something told him to look out the window.

That was when he saw movement outside. Two figures in military uniforms were rushing toward an unmarked pickup truck. One had a small, torch-like weapon strapped over his shoulder. The other one had handguns on his waist belt.

This sent Rednose into a stage of fear and self-preservation. He had to escape this situation before he got burned inside the house, but he also needed to escape with his personal information to avoid being connected to this vicious capital murder case. He quickly found his bag with his stuff inside. He looked over his shoulder to get one last look at Ebony, as if to say goodbye, before he made an attempt to escape.

He had to be careful not to get caught by the military assassins. Or had they already seen his car and watched him enter the house? Or had they left and came back with a cleanup crew? What the hell was going on here? Rednose knew it was more serious than he originally thought.

The smoke and the unexpected situation made his head spin as he went toward the front door. There was so much smoke and heat that it was becoming unbearable.

"Come on, man!" Rednose yelled in panic. The front door was on fire, and there was no way he could escape that way. So, he ran toward the back door. It was the same thing. The door was halfway covered in flames, and dark smoke made him cover his face and cough heavily. He couldn't see anymore and began to panic. The two military guys had caved in the front and back doors before they left. Rednose opened a bathroom door in a desperate need for some air. That was when he got another surprise.

"Whoa, shit!" Just like Ebony, a female was lying on her back with a towel covering her lower body. She was dead with one bullet hole between her eyes. He quickly concluded that this was Ebony's girlfriend, and she had gotten murdered while getting out the shower.

With no way out, Rednose took his weapon off his hip and ran toward Ebony's bedroom again and shot the window out. He was careful when he grabbed the blanket from under her body and used it as protection. He jumped through the window and burned his arms, but he was free.

"Man, what the fuck just happened? I gotta get the fuck out this city!" Rednose laid on the grass for only a few moments to catch his breath. The house was completely on fire now. He had barely managed to escape. He heard people screaming and crying.

"Somebody is alive! Look!" a voice said. The smoke still had Rednose slightly blinded.

"Stay calm. The help is on the way, buddy," Rednose heard another voice say.

That was enough motivation to gather his energy and rush to his vehicle to escape. The last thing he wanted was a run in with the law. The people around the house fire were trying to stop him from leaving and asking if he was okay. One white elder even tried to stand in front of his car, so he couldn't leave.

"Hey, buddy! You're not in any position to be driving…"

Click, click!

The barrel of Rednose's gun stopped his ass in mid-sentence. "Get the fuck out my way! Now!"

Rednose was finally able to drive away. He made it to the stop sign at the end of the street and couldn't take his eyes off the gruesome scene. The house Ebony was living in with her girlfriend was completely on fire now, and you could see it all the way down the block.

That was when Rednose saw a police car with sirens on quickly coming behind him from the direction of the house.

Chapter 21

At the very moment that Rednose realized the police were about to pursue him, he began to panic. Natural instinct helped him accelerate to advance and gain a nice distance on the one police car, but he knew backup had been called by radio. He was very knowledgeable about law enforcement and knew he had a very small chance to get away on all the main roads surrounding the upscale neighborhood where Ebony and her girlfriend's house was located. He could still see smoke in the rearview mirror.

You realized that your life was flashing before your eyes when all of your memories began to play in your head at the same time. Rednose had a lot going on in his head, and it was unexplainable. The most disturbing flashes were the images of all the dead opps he stepped on. Visions of Carlos, Dominique, and others were very clear. That reminded him that if he got caught right now, there was no telling what type of heat was on him. Even though he was living a lot different now, when he first got out of prison, he was living recklessly. He wanted to blame that on the drugs, but he knew the violence was just in him.

Rednose was able to make it to some back roads without seeing any backup police cars. He thought he'd lost the initial cop car until he made a sharp left and saw that the Columbus police department officer had outsmarted him by taking a short cut to meet him head on. The on-duty officer must have been assigned to this area frequently because he

HUNGRY FOR MONEY | SLIMBOS

was more advanced than Rednose so far. Now on a two way street, they were driving toward each other. The police officer was now shining bright lights as he came closer. It was almost like a game of chicken. Rednose was not about to back down. It was all or nothing for him. He had to find a way to get up out of there. Being on the scene of that execution style, double homicide would have him sitting in the county jail for over two years waiting on a bond hearing. That was how bad Muscogee County was. They were not by the book and couldn't wait for an opportunity to railroad another ex-convict.

That was just one of the issues. Rednose had both of his weapons on him and was in a new car with counterfeit license plates thanks to Coby getting his legit car towed.

Also, he had too many enemies in the city. Everybody who used to look up to him hated him now and would not hesitate to down him back for some clout. Finally, he had too many bodies and possible robbery cases that he could be linked to. So, he had no choice but to try a suicide mission.

Rednose put on his seatbelt before he swerved in the wrong lane on purpose. He hit the gas pedal to the floor and blew the horn repeatedly. At first, the police car started doing the same thing. It didn't take long to see who was bluffing. With only seconds before impact, the cop car slowed down and jumped in the opposite lane, which was the wrong one for him.

"Yeah! Motherfucker!" Rednose yelled, full of fear and adrenaline.

They locked eyes while driving past each other. Rednose was even more shocked when he noticed it was a brown-skinned, female cop.

"What the fuck?! Damn, that bitch can drive! She not playing around." Rednose smiled in excitement. Yep, he knew he was not right in the head because as bad as this situation was, he was impressed and somewhat turned on by the female's braveness.

123

But she wasn't done. It wasn't over. She immediately hit a U-turn that would have made Ludacris jealous and got behind him and continued to pursue. Rednose's smile turned to a wow face as he looked ahead and saw he had an option to merge left or make a right. Two cars were coming from the left of him. He hit his signal light as if he was going left but quickly made a right. Next, he drove as fast as he could until he saw the interstate signs. The police car was almost out of sight. He was doing the impossible — out running the police in an arena he had no win in.

When the two cars passed each other, he knew he had gained a slight advantage and did his best to get up out of there. A few minutes later, he was on the interstate, and from there, he knew she was going to radio all the state patrol. So, he wasn't going to be on there long. He just needed to get to familiar territory. He got off three exits later and blended in with the heavy traffic. His car was dark gray, so it didn't stand out too much. There was no sign of any police car. Rednose knew he had to get out of the car asap before he got out of the city altogether.

The first person he thought of was the only female he had been texting recently, and that was his own little friend he had linked back up with at the gas station. Luckily, he had been beating her back in because she picked up on the first ring.

"Baby, I'm in trouble. I just wrecked my car. I'll explain when you get here. Finna share my location so you can get here immediately." Rednose hung up after she said she was already in her car and on the way to him right now.

Just when Rednose was about to move out of the city for good, all hell broke loose. He couldn't stop thinking about Ebony. She had saved his life when he was in a circle of death. He felt in his heart that he was forever indebted to her. He stood on loyalty and loved hard when he let a person in. On the other hand, for all his opposition, they would feel his wrath. Furthermore, he would not close his business in the city until he found out who those two guys in military fits were that murdered Ebony.

Chapter 22

Nobody had heard from or seen Rednose in over a month since Ebony and her girlfriend's bodies were identified in what was left of their house. If the fire department would not have responded as fast as they had, it could have been worse. The city was shocked as the details to the gruesome double homicide were revealed. Both girls had been victims of a home invasion and were even sexually assaulted and tortured before they were both killed with a bullet to the head.

Coby was not the same person as he used to be. He had literally lost his mind after losing the only sister he knew. They shared a special relationship, and she always had his back. Now, he truly felt like he was living in a world with no family. To make matters worse, he could not get in contact with Rednose. At first, he figured that maybe Rednose had something to do with it because word on the street was he was on the run from the police. After weeks of no way to get in contact with him, Coby knew Rednose had left him for dead. His personal phone number was even disconnected. Coby even had a few of his young flunkies go check out the spot outside of the city, and they reported that no one was living there at all.

Now, Coby was on his own with free will to give orders to his team without any pushback from his sister or Rednose. This was not good news for the city of Columbus. Now, Coby was not really a bad guy at first. Living under Rednose's wing for so long and getting trained for the ongoing war had changed him. Now with his sister dead, he really was heartless. The sad part was that she was buried at the same exact cemetery that his girlfriend was, the one who Ice Water had shot to death while shooting at them both. All these events combined had turned Coby into a maniac.

He was on all the worst drugs — ice and spice. He was always high and wigging out on all of his young flunkies. He would pull out his gun on them for the simplest things. They were very afraid of him.

Let's not forget that a lot of people feared and respected him because of the publicity stunt he took credit for by dropping the video where Carlos' body was found hanging. So, nobody on his team was brave enough to put him in his place. Speaking of Carlos, the beef with the RRG (Real Right Gang) members was still ongoing. This was now Coby's beef and not Rednose's. At least that was how Coby was carrying on.

From the outside looking in, it looked like the once powerful RRG members were now ducking smoke. Coby and his team had just recently been bragging on social media that they were responsible for shooting up a party and killing two of the opps they were now smoking on. In actuality, RRG wasn't as deep as they were in the beginning. The Feds had been in town locking up the main guys all year. Coby's team just happened to be young and new. They weren't making enough noise yet to be on the Feds' radar. That would change very soon, especially with this next act Coby had up his sleeve.

Word on the street was that Ice Water was now dating Cee Money's sister. One of Coby's flunkies also used to fuck with the same hoe. So, it didn't take long for Coby to find out some information that would really set things off to another level of danger.

"Aye, Coby, where you at?" One of the guys on his team was calling him like it was important.

"Damn, nigga, you must be with the Feds or the opps trying to set me up! You asking weird ass shit like that! What's up? Why you talking so fast, nigga?" Coby was dealing with mental issues and some PTSD from all he'd been dealing with this year.

"Aye, pull up to the trap on the south, man. We got word on who sent that hit on your sister and em!" The young nigga really had Coby's attention now.

"Man, stop playing! I'm on the way now! Y'all better not be capping! I'ma free pick one of y'all fuck niggas speaking on my sister!" Coby yelled then headed to the south.

A few hours later, Coby was crying his heart out. He was sitting inside his car, staring at a picture of his sister. He had just found out what actually happened, and it had nothing to do with his sister or her girlfriend. All this shit fell back on his and Rednose's drama.

So, word had gotten back to one of Coby's flunkies named Lil Nut. Lil Nut's sister came to him after getting her hair done and spilled the tea. There were some girls gossiping about how they couldn't believe how wrong those niggas did Ebony and her girlfriend. Supposedly, it was supposed to be a robbery set up by Cee Money's sister, who was told by Cee Money that Rednose and Coby had a big stash of money and drugs ducked off that Ebony was holding on to. That was why Ebony was in her bag with all the new shit and living good in her big house and foreign car. Ice Water had followed Ebony's girl home from work one day but kept driving past the house. That was how he knew the address. It wasn't long afterwards that he sent out a blitz. The two guys he sent were both white guys with military experience. After they didn't find anything, somehow the home invasion turned into a flat out sexual assault, which led to them having no choice but to kill them and burn the house to try to hide what they did.

Coby couldn't stop the tears from falling as he crushed up shards of crystal meth and crushed it up to snort up his nose like it was cocaine. After sniffing up a big pile, he just stared at the street, looking like he was a zombie or something.

"Say, fam, you gotta stop doing that ice shit. We gonna get them…"

Blah!

Coby shot the random flunky in his head in front of everyone at the trap, shocking them completely. The flunky opened his mouth at the wrong time. Now, he was dying slow. Coby didn't even look at him. He just started yelling loudly before he drove down the street at full speed, leaving his team and surrounding junkies very afraid. Yeah, Coby had lost his got damn mind, but what he would do next would top even that.

Chapter 23

Cee Money was not the same girl that she was when Rednose first met her. Her charm had not been working on guys lately, and she had been struggling to pay her bills. Her money was so funny that she was hungry for any come up she could pull off. She was becoming desperate and willing to do anything. She didn't want to go back to being broke like the days she experienced growing up. She felt bad for getting involved with setting up the home invasion on Rednose's girl, Ebony. Honestly, she was jealous and felt like the good life that Ebony was living should have been her lifestyle if she hadn't become greedy. Her money hungry ways didn't go as planned because Rednose never had any money inside Ebony's house. So, it was a dummy mission that her and her sister had put together. Now, she felt bad after both girls ended up dead.

She knew that her sister had some niggas set it up, but she didn't know that the niggas were connected to Ice Water and the RRG members. Once she found that out, she really felt like she betrayed Rednose completely. The love she had for him was real, but the money addiction she had was stronger. Rednose would never believe that she had no choice but to set him up in order to save her sister's life. She had to make a decision, and her family would always come before any friends or man she was in love with.

"Damn, all this shit my fault," she cried as she picked up her phone and tried to reach out to Rednose. His number was disconnected or changed. She had no way to reach him.

She wanted to confess everything to him, starting from the beginning. She wanted him to know that Carlos was her man at the time they met, and the day she made Rednose believe that Carlos was robbing her, he was actually just getting his money back from her because she had run off with some bags of gas and money. Her and Carlos were on and off like that because Carlos had a bunch of side bitches. She knew she was even a side bitch but caught feelings when he began to spoil her. When Rednose got out of prison, she had stopped fucking around with Carlos, but she was still so money hungry that she knew she could use Rednose to rob him, and she would benefit.

She never expected Rednose to do what he did. She didn't know how dangerous Rednose was until Carlos' body was found hanging from a tree.

After the RRG members found out she was probably involved with Carlos' death, they snatched up her sister, and that was when she was forced to go along with the plan to set up Rednose. It didn't work, and Rednose knew she had something to do with it all. After that, she was an enemy to both sides and felt stupid. Since then, she had been trying to get back on either side, but her attempts failed. She had even faked a pregnancy, hoping to lure Rednose, but it didn't work.

Now, she was so depressed, and she had fallen to her lowest point. She had settled for the closest thing to money she could get, and that was Carlos' main shooter, Ice Water. Yeah, Cee Money's thot ass was now fucking another member of the crew. She was just a sad hoe at this point. Ice Water had even turned her back out on the yerks. She would get so freaky on the pills that she would do damn near anything for more. Her sister wasn't any better with the way she was getting run through for money and drugs. Those two freaks were fucking all the popular niggas in the city and would try to set up any one of them. This was how the youngest sister got kidnapped. Cee Money's youngest sister was only fourteen years old and a freshman in high school, so she rode the bus home from school. She was the only one of the sisters who still lived with their mother on the south side. She used to walk home from the bus stop every day with no problems until Coby got word of this.

One of Coby's flunkies had told Coby that one of Cee Money's sisters was walking home from the bus stop. "The bus stop? Man, both of them hoes grown, brah. What you talking about a bus stop?" Coby responded.

"Oh, nah. Yesterday when I was serving these Percocets outside the strip club off Victory Drive, I heard one of them hoes saying Cee Money's sisters got a video going around Facebook of her sucking her mama boyfriend dick, and the reason they knew it was the youngest sister was because she rode the bus with one of the strippers' lil brothers." Coby's flunky was laughing like he knew some sick joke.

"What's so funny, nigga?" Coby asked, getting frustrated with the childish actions.

"Man, Coby, she the best looking one. This lil hoe thick as fuck, and she got on this small ass skirt." He was still talking about her looks when Coby snapped.

"This ain't no joke, nigga! Snatch that bitch up and meet me at the trap!" Coby disconnected and sped to the trap house.

Cee Money's baby sister, Keisha, was lightheaded and dizzy. She didn't know where she was, and for a minute, she was stuck in a trance. She was blindfolded and had duct tape over her mouth. Her arms and legs were tied to something, and she couldn't get loose. She heard voices and felt hands that violated her rubbing all over her young body parts. She knew she was in trouble and couldn't scream or break free. She couldn't remember anything, and that was what frightened her the most. When she stopped screaming, she heard voices telling her to shut the fuck up before she got shot. Even at the age of fourteen, she knew what the barrel of a gun felt like on her bare skin.

"Bitch, listen to me carefully because I'm only going to say this once. Unlock your phone and call one of your sisters. Tell them if they don't show up to get you without calling the police, you will die, and we only want the nigga, Ice Water, or the same thing going to happen to you that happened to Ebony and her girlfriend."

Keisha felt her hand being freed, and her iPhone was put in her hand. She still could not see or talk. A few minutes later, she was freed of the blindfold and duct tape. All she saw was a man with a dark mask on wearing all-black. This scared the shit out of her, and she almost pissed on herself.

"Ahhhhh! Hellppppppp!" She tried to scream and get loose. This was a huge mistake because she got herself slapped and choked up.

"Bitch, shut the fuck up before I let my young niggas fuck you in your little tight ass all fucking night! If you scream again, I'ma shoot you in your face, bitch. Now, my sister got murdered and raped because of your sisters. Now you about to get the same treatment, and we going to record it since you like sucking grown man dick on Facebook!" Coby pointed his gun in her face.

"Nooo, I did not suck dick on Facebook. That was an accident! Please don't hurt me. I'll do whatever you say," she begged.

Coby made her call Cee Money and then the other sister as well. He planned on kidnapping all three of them bitches and holding them hostage until they tricked Ice Water into coming to pick them up. He was going to finally get his revenge on Ice Water once and for all.

Chapter 24

So, it all came down to this, everything that happened in the city since Rednose came home from prison. All the violence, murder, and mayhem that had been going on in the city. All the crosses, double crosses, and triple crosses. All the dead bodies and street wars. All caused by one female, Cee Money.

If Cee Money would have never met Rednose, a lot of people would still be alive, like Ebony. Ebony didn't deserve to lose her life, and she deserved justice. At least that was how her brother, Coby, felt. Lately, he had been acting like a maniac. He used drugs to deal with the depression. He didn't have many friends but had major trust issues. This wasn't how it all started in the beginning. Ebony would still be alive if Rednose would have never become a part of their lives. Coby had changed his whole personality when he started hanging around Rednose and the house him and Ebony had was shot up the first time Ebony got hit by bullets. Luckily, she survived that first shootout. However, Coby wasn't able to save her the second time. That was why he felt like he had no other choice but to get revenge by any means necessary. He didn't feel bad as he looked over at the underaged girl that was bound to the floor beneath him. That young lady was Cee Money's baby sister. Since Cee Money and Ice Water had something to do with Ebony and her girlfriend getting robbed, , and murdered, he was going to do her baby sister the same way and even worse.

Standing around and surrounding the trap house were a bunch of Coby's gang members and flunkies. They were expecting Cee Money's crew to pull up at any moment. You could hear the young girl screaming out in fear even with tape around her mouth, but Coby didn't have any mercy. He was actually thinking about letting his boys gang rape her. Why should he care? Ice Water had completely ruined his life. First of all, Coby and Ice Water were in love with the same girl. When she decided to end things with Ice Water, her and Coby were both shot by Ice Water. She died, but Coby survived. Then, Ice Water also spun the block and shot up his house and put Ebony in the hospital. Lastly, him and Cee Money were both responsible for Ebony and her girlfriend's house getting burned down. Ebony and her girlfriend were both raped and murdered. Coby felt like Rednose had abandoned them. He didn't know if Rednose was afraid or what, but at this point, he didn't give a fuck! "I am ready to die today!" said Coby. He snorted a line of powder.

Meanwhile, Cee Money was trying to hold her emotions together. She was so concerned about her baby sister's safety that she couldn't stop shaking. She had a backup plan and hoped it would work because her sister's life depended on it. All of a sudden, the car stopped, and Ice Water took his gun off safety. Him and a few of his shooters jumped out the car aggressively.

"Aye, Cee Money, call that nigga and tell em we outside."

Rednose was in disbelief as he sped down the highway. He couldn't believe the call he'd received. First, Coby and Cee Money both pled their case. Both tried to convince him to take their side. Rednose was on the way to rescue one of them. But who?

Coby heard gunshots outside the spot and instantly dropped to the floor. He heard the windows shattered by bullets. That was when he heard the girl screaming. Her voice was low because of the tape around her mouth, but he knew it was her. When the shooting stopped for a while, he ran over to her and was happy to see she wasn't shot. Next, he untied her and used her as a shield.

"Come on, lil bitch. Yo sister outside," said Coby as he held his gun to the back of her head. Coby figured Cee Money was going to bring some shooters with her, but he didn't think they were coming like that. Coby began to shoot his way through the crowd, looking for Cee Money and Ice Water.

Cee Money wasn't afraid of gunfire. This wasn't the first shootout she had been a part of. She wasn't the same person she was a year ago. She had a new purpose in life, and nobody knew her secret besides one person. This was the moment of truth. Ice Water, Coby, Cee Money, the RRG members and all of Coby's flunkies were preparing to start shooting at each other. It was about to be the biggest shootout in the city. Body after body was falling. It seemed like forever, but it was only for about twenty-four seconds.

Rednose double parked a few houses down the street from the shoutout that was taking place. He hopped out the car with his gun out. All he could think about was the look on Ebony's face with the bullet hole in her head. Revenge was a must. Rednose noticed all the bodies as he snuck through the back door. He could hear arguing coming from upstairs. The arguing coming from upstairs was from Ice Water and Coby as they exchanged gunfire. Rednose paused for about twenty-four seconds and began to daydream about everything that led up to this moment.

***

This was by far the saddest day for Rednose since he had been home from prison. One of the only females he ever had real feelings for was taken away because of him. He blamed himself for the murder of Ebony and her girlfriend. In his dreams, the images haunted him so badly. Rednose still remembered the look on her face when he found her dead in her bed with a bullet in between her eyes.

Rednose felt tears falling down his face as he replayed the day Ebony saved his life...

(Flashback)

Imagine being in the middle of a triangle, surrounded by shooters. You could either panic then become a sitting duck, or you could drop your nuts and shoot your way out of the jam. Rednose didn't have time to think. He'd been in a few shootouts before he went to prison. He was shot a couple of times, but none were life threatening. In prison, he'd been in a bunch of knife fights. He almost lost his life once before after being caught in a jam. That time, he'd panicked. Afterwards, he told himself that he would never fold up when being attacked by a group. In fact, the next time he got ambushed and was caught up in a jam, he would rush the crowd and catch them off guard. That was exactly what he did.

First, Rednose did a quick observation of his total surroundings. There was one car behind him with shooters, a shooter on foot coming from the left, and another shooter creeping from the right. He could tell they didn't know what they were doing, but it looked good if they were trying to scare somebody. The closest shooter was the one coming from the left, the same side where Cee Money was supposed to have been on a porch. Rednose hopped out, stayed low, and fired at the shooter, catching him completely off guard. He tried to run but was hit and dropped his weapon before he stumbled on the grass. Rednose ran low and fast away from the car and other shooter. He was shooting behind his back as he ran. Rednose was moving like a professional assassin. If these streets punks were smart or had any skills, they would have not let him get out the vehicle and scatter around the darkness like that. Now, it was hard to hit him. A few people that were outside were now running in all directions, which made it harder to get Rednose.

The shooter that was on foot met up with the shooter that got out of the car, and they were now standing over the shooter that Rednose shot down. Rednose saw this interaction going on from the dumpster he was hiding behind. From reading the body language, the guy he hit was probably still alive. He saw another man come out with a gun to a female's head then lead her to a car. Next, two of the shooters picked up their mans and carried him to a car that had just pulled up and put him inside. The car sped away as quickly as it pulled up. At that moment, Rednose knew he was dealing with a large group of people that pretty much had these apartments as a main base. You could tell everyone in this apartment complex ran with these guys. Rednose knew he had to get the hell out of there, or he was going to become a sitting duck. He wasn't even happy about not getting shot. All he could think about was how Cee Money set him up and sold him out like that. This had a burning feeling in his chest. It was like a part of him was hurting badly. He was filled with rage, and his heart was broken all in one.

His phone began to vibrate, which brought him out of the trance he had slid into. It was a private number, so he ignored it.

"Where the fuck she at?" he asked himself, thinking about the Plan B he had put together because he knew something wasn't right with Cee Money. He just had to actually see it to believe it, and it nearly cost him his life force. Just then, his phone rang again, and it was his backup plan.

"Yeah, meet me at the Churches across from the apartments. Okay, you already there? Good, I knew I could count on you. Yes, I'm okay. You was right about that dog ass hoe. I'ma take care of her personally, but Carlos' family and them RRG niggas finna hurt real bad after my next act. The show just getting started."

Rednose disconnected the call and checked to make sure the coast was clear before he made a dash for the wooded area. He jumped a fence and landed hard on something. "Agggghhhh, fuck!" he yelled, falling on his ass in agony. He grabbed his left ankle. He knew he had broken it or something because it swelled up instantly. He must have been making noise because he heard a few junkies coming toward him. Next, he heard a dog barking. Those two factors made him briefly ignore the pain. He ran like hell until he was across the street from the apartments. Then, he walked in pain up a dark street until he came behind the Churches' building. He saw her car at about the same time as he heard a group of niggas running toward him.

"There his bitch ass go right there! Shoot him!" a voice yelled before shots rang out.

Rednose sent shots back to buy more time. The shooters didn't stop their pursuit. They just ducked down when he shot back. Fortunately, Rednose was able to jump inside the getaway car before the shooters were anywhere near hitting him. As they drove away, one bullet hit the back bumper but didn't cause any real damage. It only made the driver's survival skills kick in, and she got them to safety.

"You good, boo?" the light-skinned girl with the long, reddish colored dreadlocks asked him as she got on the interstate.

"Yeah, take me to my spot so I can pack all my shit. That bitch knows where I stay. I'm moving out," Rednose reluctantly stated. You could hear defeat in his voice.

The female driver noticed that also. She saw the sadness and shame all over his face. While he was usually joyful and confident, at the moment, he looked very weak and confused.

The female's name was Ebony, and she was Rednose's female friend.

This was the day Rednose and Ebony began an unbreakable bond. Now, she was gone, and Rednose would make sure she had closure for damn sure.

***

There were still no suspects arrested, but that was because the military assassins that took up the hit on Ebony and her girlfriend were both dead corpses now. Rednose knew it wasn't going to take him long to get revenge, especially with the help of someone he had been secretly creeping with on the low.

Although Rednose was not feeling Ebony having the police pull up to the spot out of town, making him second guess her loyalty, he was still in love with her. She was not a street girl, just trying to fit in to be down for him. Her whole style was nonchalant about most things the average girl demanded. Her personality was laidback. Her smile could brighten up the entire room. She always had a positive vibe. Rednose was thinking of all the small details he missed about her now that she was gone. The way he walked down on her killers displayed his true feelings for Ebony.

He knew after finding out about her and Coby being more than fake brother and sister that it would never be the same anyway. She could have at least kept that part honest with Rednose. Now that she was dead, he would never receive true closure on the situation.

There were signs he noticed when they all lived together in the house outside of the city. Coby had begun to act weird once Rednose and Ebony grew closer. Rednose used to treat Coby like the baby brother he never had. After Coby experienced a few shootouts and started playing with his nose, Rednose decided to slowly create space. Coby had began moving very carelessly. Stupid shit like that could have the Feds all on Rednose's ass.

Honestly, Rednose was supposed to have gotten rid of Coby when his dumb ass decided to shoot a fucking video where Carlos' body went viral. Yet he spared him and just continued to teach him how to move. Also, Rednose needed a dummy to help him go on his missions after things went left with Cee Money. He even made him feel like a part of his team by calling them RRG Killers.

Coby took that and ran with it. He was clout chasing so hard that he failed to realize Rednose was using him as a pawn on his chess board. If Coby would have passed all of Rednose's tests, he would have accepted him as a hardheaded little brother who just needed some coaching and someone to teach him the game of life. But all that changed once Rednose took a trip to Cali, and Coby betrayed him.

Rednose knew Coby would try to go back to the city while he was out of the state. Coby thought Rednose didn't have eyes and ears in the city, but he was so naive. That was why when Coby called Rednose from the county jail, he sent his stupid ass to voicemail. Coby fell for the bait.

The day Coby put an expiration date on his life was when he dropped his little nut sack and attacked Rednose then made threats of pistol play.

***

(*Flashback*)
Later on that night, Ebony and Rednose were lying in bed together, watching a movie on Netflix. Ebony's phone began ringing, so she answered.

"Hey, what's going on?" Ebony listened to the caller then said, "Okay, I'm coming."

Rednose decided to check his accounts while Ebony walked out of the room. Rednose didn't hear or see it coming. He was actually more shocked than hurt.

"What's up? Fight back! I've been waiting for this day. I knew I was going to catch you down bad. I've been laying on your bitch ass," yelled Coby as he ambushed Rednose with a flurry of punches.

Okay, so let's unpack this. Coby had called Ebony to open the door once he rode past her girlfriend's house and noticed someone else was there. He didn't know it was Rednose until he walked inside. All the rage and hatred he had immediately came out. He was very emotional and upset. It was funny he felt that way now because a few months ago, he felt the total opposite way about Rednose.

"That's all you got, nigga! You hit like a bitch!" Rednose said in between punches. Because he was under the cover when he was ambushed, he was not in a position to fight back, so all he could do at the moment was take the punches and trash talk.

Ebony was trying to get Coby to get off Rednose. Rednose was much stronger than Coby. Yet he was under a blanket. Coby wasn't weak and was big for his age, so it took a little effort to get out the awkward position. Once Rednose got up, he threw Coby across the room.

"My mouth bleeding! Oh, I'm finna beat your lil bitch ass, boy. I don't know what the fuck your problem is, and I been trying to spare yo lil police ass because I know you don't know any better!" Rednose began stomping and kicking Coby all in his face. Coby tried to stop the kicks, but Rednose was becoming more vicious with each kick.

Ebony was screaming for him to stop. When she saw he wasn't paying her any attention, she ran into the kitchen and grabbed a big pot. Without even thinking about it, she ran back inside the room and began swinging it in Rednose's direction. She hit him a few times in the back of the head.

"Ouch! Bitch, you crazy! Why the fuck you swinging that big ass pot at me like you lost yo motherfuckin mind?" Rednose grabbed the back of his head and rubbed the big ass knot that popped up instantly. He was also sweating and kind of out of breath. It had been months since he'd been to the gym, and at that moment, he realized he was out of shape.

"Coby, you have to leave now!" Ebony yelled, helping him up. Ebony was talking under her breath and was clearly frustrated.

"I'ma see you again! Next time, we not doing no fighting!" Coby yelled as he rushed out.

"Next time? No fighting? Nigga, what's up? You talking about gun smoke? You not bout that life! You little young ass street punk! Matter of fact…"

Rednose went from mad to outrageously angry after Coby had just made a threat in his face.

He rushed behind Coby and went to his car and went under his seat to grab his gun. Next, he popped the trunk and got his emergency weapon. He walked over to Coby, who was trying to get in his car and leave. He passed him one of the guns and just stared at him.

"Oh, my goodness! No, Rednose! Please! What are y'all doing?" Ebony was crying as she watched Coby and Rednose stare each other down, each pointing a weapon at the other.

Ebony didn't want it to come to this or come out in this way; however, she knew what Coby was going to do before he did it.

"You right. I'm not about that life. Here, you get your gun back. I don't want no problems." Coby was smiling in a slick way, like he knew a secret. He got in his car and began to leave.

Rednose put his guns away and stared at Ebony with surprise. He rubbed his knot again. He was about to say something to her until Coby stopped and yelled out his window a few words that would change everything Rednose thought he knew about Ebony.

"Rednose, if I was you, I would not be in the city, nigga. Everybody wants yo head. You came down here into a death trap just to chase behind a piece of pussy. Ebony, did you show Rednose that trick you do when you on top? This hoe got you so blind you had no idea we been fucking since day one. Your duck ass went for the brother and sister bullshit. You would of been better off with that money hungry slut, Cee Money. Now who laughing, fuck nigga? Go put some ice on that knot, duck ass nigga." Coby sped away, blasting drill music.

***

Coby felt like Rednose was kind of the reason Ebony was dead. Rednose knew that was not the case. However, he wasn't going to explain shit to nobody. Actually, Ebony was dead because of the same reason Coby's girlfriend was dead. Ice Water, Carlos' main shooter. Rednose knew everything about the entire setup. Why did he know? Because he had planted a mole in his opps 'camp. The truth was all about to hit the fan. This was the day Rednose decided to wrap up this war in the city because he had bigger and better things to do. This whole situation wasn't even part of his plans. It seemed like all this shit took place in twenty-four seconds, like a shot clock.

Once all this petty shit was over, Rednose would go back to his plans he had setup before he even came home from prison. These plans included revenge and closure. His hunger for money was still there, but he wasn't anywhere near broke. However, he had to start a new saving account soon, not for him but for his son.

"Wassup, pussy ass nigga? Pop out!" yelled Ice Water as he shot in Coby's direction. He had two handguns and was firing each pistol one after the other. This clown ass nigga thought he was in a movie or something. He was being all extra, doing unnecessary movement, which would be a fatal mistake. If he would have gone ahead and just flat-out blitzed Coby, he could have finally put an end to this war between them once and for all, but he wanted to be fancy. Ice Water was shooting wildly and randomly. This made

Coby drop to the ground and return fire. Coby was low but moving swiftly.

"You killed my girl and my sister, bitch ass nigga!" said Coby. They continued to shout at each other for about twenty-four seconds. Meanwhile, both of their fellow teammates were taking each other out, bullet for bullet. The gunfire was so loud, and shots were wild. None of these guys had ever been in a real shootout.

This was some crazy shit, but this was exactly the type of gun violence that claimed lives every day in our community. Bullets didn't have a name, and a wannabe shooter didn't have any aim. This was the only upper hand that Coby had on the others. Rednose had him going to shooting ranges every weekend in the early days when he first took Coby under his wing. Coby didn't know back then that the training course would be essential. Coby was able to hit several of the shooters trying to close in on him, but Ice Water just kept ducking and dodging. Not only was Ice Water hard to kill, but he was also not trying to ease up. He kept the pressure on Coby. Coby knew he couldn't hold him off any longer, so he decided to go out with a bang. Just when he was about to stand up and go out guns blazing, he noticed someone appear directly behind Ice Water.

Rednose emerged out of nowhere, pointing the barrel of his gun at the back of Ice Water's head. "You don't look so cool now, Ice Water."

BOW!

Everyone was shocked to see Ice Water's body drop to the ground after Rednose put a bullet in the back of his head! It seemed like Rednose popped up out of nowhere, like a superhero!

"That was for Ebony, nigga!" yelled Rednose, standing over Ice Water's dead body. There was a brief moment of silence when Coby and Rednose's eyes met each other. The stare down was so intense. For twenty-four seconds, they locked eyes! Cee Money used this opportunity to go rescue her sister. But Coby saw her and started chasing behind her. Rednose saw him and started chasing behind him. Just when Cee Money got close to her sister, Coby grabbed her. He pointed his gun in her face.

"Now what, bitch?" yelled Coby with tears in his eyes. He gripped his gun tighter. "Snake ass bitch, you set my sister up. I'm finna kill you!" Coby was about to squeeze the trigger until he felt some cold steel on the back of his head.

In a calm voice, Rednose tried to warn him. "DROP THE GUN, MY G."

Coby couldn't believe his ears. Why would Rednose take Cee Money's side? Coby was so confused. His eyes jumped from Cee Money to Rednose. Coby was experiencing the element of surprise. It seemed like they were hiding secrets. Ebony had to be rolling in her grave. Cody wasn't about to let shit end like this.

"OH, HELL NAWL!"

Just when Coby was about to pull the trigger, Rednose shot him in the back of the head. Coby was dead twenty-four seconds later. Rednose walked out with his baby mama, Cee Money!?!

Wow!

TO BE CONTINUED
Part 2 Coming Soon.
Stay tuned.
Hungry For Money: 24 Seconds
via Lockdown Publications

Lock Down Publications and Ca$h Presents
Assisted Publishing Packages

BASIC PACKAGE $499 Editing Cover Design Formatting	UPGRADED PACKAGE $800 Typing Editing Cover Design Formatting
ADVANCE PACKAGE $1,200 Typing Editing Cover Design Formatting Copyright registration Proofreading Upload book to Amazon	LDP SUPREME PACKAGE $1,500 Typing Editing Cover Design Formatting Copyright registration Proofreading Set up Amazon account Upload book to Amazon Advertise on LDP, Amazon and Facebook Page

***Other services available upon request.
Additional charges may apply

Lock Down Publications
P.O. Box 944
Stockbridge, GA 30281-9998
Phone: 470 303-9761

Submission Guideline

Submit the first three chapters of your completed manuscript to ldpsubmissions@gmail.com. In the subject line add **Your Book's Title**. The manuscript must be in a Word Doc file and sent as an attachment. Document should be in Times New Roman, double spaced, and in size 12 font. Also, provide your synopsis and full contact information. If sending multiple submissions, they must each be in a separate email.

Have a story but no way to send it electronically? You can still submit to LDP/Ca$h Presents. Send in the first three chapters, written or typed, of your completed manuscript to:

LDP: Submissions Dept
P.O. Box 944
Stockbridge, GA 30281-9998

DO NOT send original manuscript. Must be a duplicate.
Provide your synopsis and a cover letter containing your full contact information.

Thanks for considering LDP and Ca$h Presents.

NEW RELEASES

BLOODLINE OF A SAVAGE 1&2
THESE VICIOUS STREETS 1&2
RELENTLESS GOON
RELENTLESS GOON 2
BY PRINCE A. TAUHID

THE BUTTERFLY MAFIA 1-3
BY FUMIYA PAYNE

A THUG'S STREET PRINCESS 1&2
BY MEESHA

CITY OF SMOKE 2
BY MOLOTTI

STEPPERS 1,2&3
THE REAL BADDIES OF CHI-RAQ
BY KING RIO

THE LANE 1&2
BY KEN-KEN SPENCE

THUG OF SPADES 1&2
LOVE IN THE TRENCHES 2
CORNER BOYS
BY COREY ROBINSON

TIL DEATH 3
BY ARYANNA

THE BIRTH OF A GANGSTER 4
BY DELMONT PLAYER

PRODUCT OF THE STREETS 1&2
BY DEMOND "MONEY" ANDERSON

NO TIME FOR ERROR
BY KEESE

MONEY HUNGRY DEMONS
BY TRANAY ADAMS

Coming Soon from Lock Down Publications/Ca$h Presents

IF YOU CROSS ME ONCE 6
ANGEL V
By Anthony Fields

IMMA DIE BOUT MINE 5
By Aryanna

A THUGS STREET PRINCESS 3
By Meesha

PRODUCT OF THE STREETS 3
By Demond Money Anderson

CORNER BOYS 2
By Corey Robinson

THE MURDER QUEENS 6&7
By Michael Gallon

CITY OF SMOKE 3
By Molotti

CONFESSIONS OF A DOPE BOY
By Nicholas Lock

THA TAKEOVER
By Keith Chandler

BETRAYAL OF A G 2
By Ray Vinci

CRIME BOSS
By Playa Ray

Available Now

RESTRAINING ORDER 1 & 2
By **CA$H & Coffee**

LOVE KNOWS NO BOUNDARIES 1-3
By **Coffee**

RAISED AS A GOON I, II, III & IV
BRED BY THE SLUMS I, II, III
BLAST FOR ME I & II
ROTTEN TO THE CORE I II III
A BRONX TALE I, II, III
DUFFLE BAG CARTEL I II III IV V VI
HEARTLESS GOON I II III IV V
A SAVAGE DOPEBOY I II
DRUG LORDS I II III
CUTTHROAT MAFIA I II
KING OF THE TRENCHES
By **Ghost**

LAY IT DOWN I & II
LAST OF A DYING BREED I II
BLOOD STAINS OF A SHOTTA I & II III
By **Jamaica**

LOYAL TO THE GAME I II III
LIFE OF SIN I, II III
By **TJ & Jelissa**

IF LOVING HIM IS WRONG…I & II
LOVE ME EVEN WHEN IT HURTS I II III
By **Jelissa**

PUSH IT TO THE LIMIT
By **Bre' Hayes**

BLOODY COMMAS I & II
SKI MASK CARTEL I, II & III
KING OF NEW YORK I II, III IV V
RISE TO POWER I II III
COKE KINGS I II III IV V
BORN HEARTLESS I II III IV
KING OF THE TRAP I II
By **T.J. Edwards**

WHEN THE STREETS CLAP BACK I & II III
THE HEART OF A SAVAGE I II III IV
MONEY MAFIA I II
LOYAL TO THE SOIL I II III
By **Jibril Williams**

A DISTINGUISHED THUG STOLE MY HEART I II & III
LOVE SHOULDN'T HURT I II III IV
RENEGADE BOYS 1-4
PAID IN KARMA 1-3
SAVAGE STORMS 1-3
AN UNFORESEEN LOVE 1-3
BABY, I'M WINTERTIME COLD 1-3
A THUG'S STREET PRINCESS 1&2
By **Meesha**

A GANGSTER'S CODE 1-3
A GANGSTER'S SYN 1-3
THE SAVAGE LIFE 1-3
CHAINED TO THE STREETS 1-3
BLOOD ON THE MONEY 1-3
A GANGSTA'S PAIN 1-3
BEAUTIFUL LIES AND UGLY TRUTHS
CHURCH IN THESE STREETS
By **J-Blunt**

CUM FOR ME 1-8
An LDP Erotica Collaboration

BLOOD OF A BOSS 1-5
SHADOWS OF THE GAME
TRAP BASTARD
By **Askari**

THE STREETS BLEED MURDER 1-3
THE HEART OF A GANGSTA 1-3
By **Jerry Jackson**

WHEN A GOOD GIRL GOES BAD
By **Adrienne**

THE COST OF LOYALTY 1-3
By **Kweli**

BRIDE OF A HUSTLA 1-3
THE FETTI GIRLS 1-3
CORRUPTED BY A GANGSTA 1-4
BLINDED BY HIS LOVE
THE PRICE YOU PAY FOR LOVE 1-3
DOPE GIRL MAGIC 1-3
By **Destiny Skai**

A KINGPIN'S AMBITION
A KINGPIN'S AMBITION II
I MURDER FOR THE DOUGH
By **Ambitious**

TRUE SAVAGE 1-7
DOPE BOY MAGIC 1-3
MIDNIGHT CARTEL 1-3
CITY OF KINGZ 1&2
NIGHTMARE ON SILENT AVE
THE PLUG OF LIL MEXICO 1&2
CLASSIC CITY
By **Chris Green**

A GANGSTER'S REVENGE 1-4
THE BOSS MAN'S DAUGHTERS 1-5
A SAVAGE LOVE 1&2
BAE BELONGS TO ME 1&2
A HUSTLER'S DECEIT 1-3
WHAT BAD BITCHES DO 1-3
SOUL OF A MONSTER 1-3
KILL ZONE
A DOPE BOY'S QUEEN 1-3
TIL DEATH 1-3
IMMA DIE BOUT MINE 1-4
By **Aryanna**

A DOPEBOY'S PRAYER
By **Eddie "Wolf" Lee**

THE KING CARTEL 1-3
By **Frank Gresham**

THESE NIGGAS AIN'T LOYAL 1-3
By **Nikki Tee**

GANGSTA SHYT 1-3
By **CATO**

THE ULTIMATE BETRAYAL
By **Phoenix**

BOSS'N UP 1-3
By **Royal Nicole**

I LOVE YOU TO DEATH
By **Destiny J**

I RIDE FOR MY HITTA
I STILL RIDE FOR MY HITTA
By **Misty Holt**

LOVE & CHASIN' PAPER
By **Qay Crockett**

TO DIE IN VAIN
SINS OF A HUSTLA
By **ASAD**

BROOKLYN HUSTLAZ
By **Boogsy Morina**

BROOKLYN ON LOCK 1 & 2
By **Sonovia**

GANGSTA CITY
By **Teddy Duke**

A DRUG KING AND HIS DIAMOND 1-3
A DOPEMAN'S RICHES
HER MAN, MINE'S TOO 1&2
CASH MONEY HO'S
THE WIFEY I USED TO BE 1&2
PRETTY GIRLS DO NASTY THINGS
By **Nicole Goosby**

LIPSTICK KILLAH 1-3
CRIME OF PASSION 1-3
FRIEND OR FOE 1-3
By **Mimi**

TRAPHOUSE KING 1-3
KINGPIN KILLAZ 1-3
STREET KINGS 1&2
PAID IN BLOOD 1&2
CARTEL KILLAZ 1-3
DOPE GODS 1&2
By **Hood Rich**

THE STREETS ARE CALLING
By **Duquie Wilson**

STEADY MOBBN' 1-3
THE STREETS STAINED MY SOUL 1-3
By **Marcellus Allen**

WHO SHOT YA 1-3
SON OF A DOPE FIEND 1-4
HEAVEN GOT A GHETTO 1&2
SKI MASK MONEY 1&2
By **Renta**

GORILLAZ IN THE BAY 1-4
TEARS OF A GANGSTA 1/&2
3X KRAZY 1&2
STRAIGHT BEAST MODE 1&2
By **DE'KARI**

TRIGGADALE 1-3
MURDA WAS THE CASE 1-3
By **Elijah R. Freeman**

SLAUGHTER GANG 1-3
RUTHLESS HEART 1-3
By **Willie Slaughter**

GOD BLESS THE TRAPPERS 1-3
THESE SCANDALOUS STREETS 1-3
FEAR MY GANGSTA 1-5
THESE STREETS DON'T LOVE NOBODY 1-2
BURY ME A G 1-5
A GANGSTA'S EMPIRE 1-4
THE DOPEMAN'S BODYGAURD 1&2
THE REALEST KILLAZ 1-3
THE LAST OF THE OGS 1-3
By **Tranay Adams**

MARRIED TO A BOSS 1-3
By **Destiny Skai & Chris Green**

KINGZ OF THE GAME 1-7
CRIME BOSS 1-3
By **Playa Ray**

FUK SHYT
By **Blakk Diamond**

DON'T F#CK WITH MY HEART 1&2
By **Linnea**

ADDICTED TO THE DRAMA 1-3
IN THE ARM OF HIS BOSS
By **Jamila**

LOYALTY AIN'T PROMISED 1&2
By **Keith Williams**

YAYO 1-4
A SHOOTER'S AMBITION 1&2
BRED IN THE GAME
By **S. Allen**

TRAP GOD 1-3
RICH $AVAGE 1-3
MONEY IN THE GRAVE 1-3
CARTEL MONEY
By **Martell Troublesome Bolden**

FOREVER GANGSTA 1&2
GLOCKS ON SATIN SHEETS 1&2
By **Adrian Dulan**

TOE TAGZ 1-4
LEVELS TO THIS SHYT 1&2
IT'S JUST ME AND YOU
By **Ah'Million**

KINGPIN DREAMS 1-3
RAN OFF ON DA PLUG
By **Paper Boi Rari**

THE STREETS MADE ME 1-3
By **Larry D. Wright**

CONFESSIONS OF A GANGSTA 1-4
CONFESSIONS OF A JACKBOY 1-3
CONFESSIONS OF A HITMAN
By **Nicholas Lock**

I'M NOTHING WITHOUT HIS LOVE
SINS OF A THUG
TO THE THUG I LOVED BEFORE
A GANGSTA SAVED XMAS
IN A HUSTLER I TRUST
By **Monet Dragun**

QUIET MONEY 1-3
THUG LIFE 1-3
EXTENDED CLIP 1&2
A GANGSTA'S PARADISE
By **Trai'Quan**

CAUGHT UP IN THE LIFE 1-3
THE STREETS NEVER LET GO 1-3
By **Robert Baptiste**

NEW TO THE GAME 1-3
MONEY, MURDER & MEMORIES 1-3
By **Malik D. Rice**

CREAM 2-3
THE STREETS WILL TALK
By **Yolanda Moore**

THE STREETS WILL NEVER CLOSE 1-3
By **K'ajji**

LIFE OF A SAVAGE 1-4
A GANGSTA'S QUR'AN 1-4
MURDA SEASON 1-3
GANGLAND CARTEL 1-3
CHI'RAQ GANGSTAS 1-4
KILLERS ON ELM STREET 1-3
JACK BOYZ N DA BRONX 1-3
A DOPEBOY'S DREAM 1-3
JACK BOYS VS DOPE BOYS 1-3
COKE GIRLZ
COKE BOYS
SOSA GANG 1&2
BRONX SAVAGES
BODYMORE KINGPINS
BLOOD OF A GOON
By **Romell Tukes**

CONCRETE KILLA 1-3
VICIOUS LOYALTY 1-3
By **Kingpen**

THE ULTIMATE SACRIFICE 1-6
KHADIFI
IF YOU CROSS ME ONCE 1-3
ANGEL 1-4
IN THE BLINK OF AN EYE
By **Anthony Fields**

THE LIFE OF A HOOD STAR
By **Ca$h & Rashia Wilson**

NIGHTMARES OF A HUSTLA 1-3
BLOOD AND GAMES 1&2
By **King Dream**

GHOST MOB
By **Stilloan Robinson**

HARD AND RUTHLESS 1&2
MOB TOWN 251
THE BILLIONAIRE BENTLEYS 1-3
REAL G'S MOVE IN SILENCE
By **Von Diesel**

MOB TIES 1-7
SOUL OF A HUSTLER, HEART OF A KILLER 1-3
GORILLAZ IN THE TRENCHES
By **SayNoMore**

BODYMORE MURDERLAND 1-3
THE BIRTH OF A GANGSTER 1-4
By **Delmont Player**

FOR THE LOVE OF A BOSS 1&2
By **C. D. Blue**

KILLA KOUNTY 1-5
By **Khufu**

MOBBED UP 1-4
THE BRICK MAN 1-5
THE COCAINE PRINCESS 1-10
STEPPERS 1-3
SUPER GREMLIN 1-4
By **King Rio**

MONEY GAME 1&2
By **Smoove Dolla**

A GANGSTA'S KARMA 1-4
By **FLAME**

KING OF THE TRENCHES 1-3
By **GHOST & TRANAY ADAMS**

HUNGRY FOR MONEY | SLIMBOS

QUEEN OF THE ZOO 1&2
By **Black Migo**

GRIMEY WAYS 1-3
BETRAYAL OF A G
By **Ray Vinci**

XMAS WITH AN ATL SHOOTER
By **Ca$h & Destiny Skai**

KING KILLA 1&2
By **Vincent "Vitto" Holloway**

BETRAYAL OF A THUG 1&2
By **Fre$h**

THE MURDER QUEENS 1-5
By **Michael Gallon**

FOR THE LOVE OF BLOOD 1-4
By **Jamel Mitchell**

HOOD CONSIGLIERE 1&2
NO TIME FOR ERROR
By **Keese**

PROTÉGÉ OF A LEGEND 1&2
LOVE IN THE TRENCHES 1&2
By **Corey Robinson**

THE PLUG'S RUTHLESS DAUGHTER
By **Tony Daniels**

BORN IN THE GRAVE 1-3
CRIME PAYS
By **Self Made Tay**

MOAN IN MY MOUTH
By **XTASY**

TORN BETWEEN A GANGSTER AND A GENTLEMAN
By **J-BLUNT & Miss Kim**

LOYALTY IS EVERYTHING 1-3
CITY OF SMOKE 1&2
By **Molotti**

HERE TODAY GONE TOMORROW 1&2
By **Fly Rock**

WOMEN LIE MEN LIE 1-4
FIFTY SHADES OF SNOW 1-3
STACK BEFORE YOU SPLURGE
GIRLS FALL LIKE DOMINOES
NAÏVE TO THE STREETS
By **ROY MILLIGAN**

PILLOW PRINCESS
By **S. Hawkins**

THE BUTTERFLY MAFIA 1-3
SALUTE MY SAVAGERY 1&2
By **Fumiya Payne**

THE LANE 1&2
By Ken-Ken Spence

THE PUSSY TRAP 1-5
By **Nene Capri**

DIRTY DNA
By **Blaque**

SANCTIFIED AND HORNY
by **XTASY**

BOOKS BY LDP'S CEO, CA$H

TRUST IN NO MAN
TRUST IN NO MAN 2
TRUST IN NO MAN 3
BONDED BY BLOOD
SHORTY GOT A THUG
THUGS CRY
THUGS CRY 2
THUGS CRY 3
TRUST NO BITCH
TRUST NO BITCH 2
TRUST NO BITCH 3
TIL MY CASKET DROPS
RESTRAINING ORDER
RESTRAINING ORDER 2
IN LOVE WITH A CONVICT
LIFE OF A HOOD STAR
XMAS WITH AN ATL SHOOTER